Opening the Happy Ever After Agency is a dream come true for co-owners Harriet, Emilia, Alexandra and Amber. London's newest bespoke concierge service offers clients everything they could possibly wish for!

Their professional lives are finally on track, but their personal lives are about to be turned upside down...by four handsome men who will whisk them away to every corner of the globe, and present them with the proposals of a lifetime!

Find out Harriet's story in

Honeymooning with Her Brazilian Boss

Discover Emilia's story in

Cinderella's Secret Royal Fling

Read Alexandra's story in

Reawakened by His Christmas Kiss

Available now!

Dear Reader,

Welcome to Blakeley Castle. For centuries it was the home of the scandalous Beaumont family until one scandal too many toppled them; for a decade the castle has been closed and the daughter of the house, wild child and infamous It Girl, Lady Lola Beaumont, lost...

Now, ten years later, the gardener's boy, Finn Hawkin, has returned to Blakeley, and this time he's in charge, when he glimpses a woman who reminds him of Lola. She may have a different name, but he'd recognize his childhood friend and first love anywhere. Will bringing the last Beaumont back to Blakeley give him the resolution he needs, or will the stirring of old emotions remind him of the girl he used to love? As for Alex, she put Lola behind her long ago. The last thing she needs is to be confronted with her past and the man who broke her heart.

Alex has been an enigma during the first two Fairytale Brides books and it's been an absolute joy to discover her secrets. I've loved writing her story. I hope you love reading it just as much.

Love,

Jessica

Reawakened by His Christmas Kiss

—

Jessica Gilmore

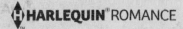

Recycling programs
for this product may
not exist in your area.

ISBN-13: 978-1-335-49964-6

Reawakened by His Christmas Kiss

First North American publication 2019

Copyright © 2019 by Jessica Gilmore

Printed in U.S.A.

A former au pair, bookseller, marketing manager and seafront trader, **Jessica Gilmore** now works for an environmental charity in York, England. Married with one daughter, one fluffy dog and two dog-loathing cats, she spends her time avoiding housework and can usually be found with her nose in a book. Jessica writes emotional romance with a hint of humor, a splash of sunshine and a great deal of delicious food—and equally delicious heroes!

Books by Jessica Gilmore

Harlequin Romance

Fairytale Brides

Honeymooning with Her Brazilian Boss
Cinderella's Secret Royal Fling

Wedding Island

Baby Surprise for the Spanish Billionaire

Summer at Villa Rosa

A Proposal from the Crown Prince

Maids Under the Mistletoe

Her New Year Baby Secret

The Life Swap

In the Boss's Castle
Unveiling the Bridesmaid

The Sheikh's Pregnant Bride
Summer Romance with the Italian Tycoon

Visit the Author Profile page
at Harlequin.com for more titles.

For Rose, Rich, Ol and Jake.
Thank you for everything.

Praise for
Jessica Gilmore

"The story is well developed...the emotions make
you feel the story and breathe life into the pages.
This is a wonderful love story sure to bring a smile
to your heart."

PROLOGUE

FINN HAWKIN ACCEPTED a glass of champagne from a passing waiter and surveyed the scene before him, his lips curving into an appreciative smile. Fairy lights and gossamer white drapes, elaborate costumes and a vast ballroom might be wasted on him, but his small nieces would want to hear about every single detail of the night. The Armarian Midsummer Ball was like every one of their favourite fairy-tales brought to life.

A masked and cloaked figure paused beside him. 'Having fun?'

'Laurent!' Finn turned to greet his old friend with genuine delight. His presence here might be more business than personal, but it was good to see his host. 'Thanks for the invite.'

'You are more than welcome. I'm glad you could come.'

A hint of sympathy tinged the other man's voice; Finn didn't confide in many people, but

Laurent knew how difficult the last year had been, the hard choices Finn had been faced with.

'How are your nieces?'

'Tired out after a week of enjoying your glorious beaches. Not that they'll admit it. Tonight they are most put out at not coming with me to a real-life royal ball. I've promised to smuggle cake back to the villa. Hopefully that will mollify them.'

'Bring them to the palace,' Laurent offered. 'It'll still be chaotic tomorrow, but maybe the day after? We have puppies in the stables they can meet, and I'll take them to the highest turret and tell them grisly stories about how my ancestors repelled would-be invaders.'

'They'll like that. Thanks, Laurent.'

'And we can catch up properly. It'll be easier when I'm not hosting several hundred people.'

'Perils of being a prince.'

But Finn couldn't help noticing that Laurent seemed more at ease than usual. He was usually so reserved, so rigid when in public, but this evening he was like a different man, his smile genuine and easy, his whole being infused with a lightness and joy that Finn couldn't imagine feeling.

'Who's the girl?'

'What girl?' Laurent's grin only widened, his eyes softening as they rested on a slim figure in yellow and silver, standing to the side of the ballroom, directing a group of waitresses.

'The girl you haven't been able to take your eyes off all night. When you haven't been disappearing outside with her, that is.'

It was unlike Laurent to be openly seen with a woman—and, although his costume gave him a degree of anonymity, it wasn't enough of a disguise to ensure complete privacy. No, if Laurent was dancing, flirting and holding intense, smouldering conversations so publicly, then his intentions must be pretty serious, and that was unexpected from a man who had seemed reconciled to a sensible marriage of convenience.

'That's Emilia. She's the party planner. She put this whole ball together in less than a month.' Laurent might have been aiming for offhand, but the pride in his voice was a dead giveaway; he was in deep.

'She's done a great job. The whole evening is magical.'

'Says the man standing on the side alone. I didn't expect you to use your plus one, Finn, but there are plenty of beautiful women here who I'm sure would love to dance with you.

Would you like me to introduce you to anyone? How about the Contessa, over there?' Laurent indicated a haughty blonde waving a fan as she ignored an eager crowd of young men.

Finn laughed. 'She looks a little above my pay grade.'

'Modesty doesn't become you, Finn. You're young, active, and you still have all your own hair and teeth. That puts you above half the men in this room, and that's before we take into account your very successful company and the small fact that you've just bought your own castle. Even the Contessa would think that makes you very suitable for one dance at least.'

'Blakeley hardly compares with a royal palace,' Finn protested, but pride swelled through him at the thought of the ancient old building, currently being restored to make a home for his nieces and a base for his rapidly expanding business.

He hadn't inherited the castle, he'd bought it with money he'd earned the hard way. Although he'd grown up on the Blakeley estate, nothing had been handed to him. His success was down to pure hard work and some lucky—and canny—decisions.

'I'm happy for you,' Laurent said softly.

'You've achieved your goal. How many men can say that?'

Finn sipped his drink. Laurent was right. He was barely thirty and he'd hit every one of the goals he'd set when they were students in Paris: to found his own business, make a fortune, and live on an estate like the one he'd grown up on. Only this time he'd be the one in the big house, not the gardener's boy, doffing his cap to his so-called betters.

'We never stop setting goals, Laurent, we just change the goalposts. Now my nieces come first. Giving them the kind of happiness and security they need…that's my priority.'

'If anyone can, you can.'

They stood there in silence for a moment, watching the opulently adorned dancers waltz around the dance floor until Laurent's gaze strayed once again to the girl in the yellow dress. Finn followed his gaze. She had moved away from the waitresses and was talking animatedly to a tall, elegant woman dressed in a demure black dress, her light brown hair elegantly coiled into a chignon.

Recognition punched him. It couldn't be…

Or could it? Was this the girl he'd searched for in vain through the years, right here in a ballroom hundreds of miles away from the place where they'd grown up?

Last time he had seen her, her hair had been bleached platinum blonde and cut into a choppy bob which had instantly spawned a thousand imitations. She'd been a decade younger, coltish and angular, with cheekbones sharp enough to cut through butter and a knowing, slanting gaze that had pouted down from billboards and magazine covers across the globe—before she had disappeared from public view and from his life, as if she had never been.

'Lola?' he half whispered. And, as if she'd heard him, the woman looked up, alert, scenting danger.

He must be imagining things. Lola Beaumont was gone, disappeared into the ether. He knew that. He'd looked for her for long enough. He blinked and refocussed. He must be mistaken. The woman was clearly working at the event, and Lola was always the guest of honour, not the help. It was a passing resemblance, that was all.

He'd thought he'd cured himself of seeing Lola at every corner years ago. But Finn couldn't stop himself from turning to Laurent. 'Who is that? Talking to Emilia?'

'Who? Oh, that's Alex—Alexandra Davenport. She co-owns a party planning agency with Emilia and two other women. She arrived yesterday, I think, to oversee things tonight so Emilia could attend the ball. Why?' Laurent's smile turned sly. 'Would you like an introduction to her?'

'No, thanks. Just curious.'

But Finn's mind was working furiously. Alexandra was Lola's middle name, wasn't it? Surely it was a coincidence—a similarity of features, a shared name, that was all. But as he gazed across at the woman he couldn't help feeling that there were no such things as coincidences and now, just as his life was exactly where he wanted it to be, Lola Beaumont had returned to disrupt it all over again.

The question was, what was he going to do about it?

CHAPTER ONE

WITH A HERCULEAN effort, Alexandra Davenport managed to wait until she had passed through Passport Control before she turned on her phone. Pulling her small case behind her, she headed towards Customs and the exit, impatient as her phone whirred through its settings and began to process all communications from the last eight hours.

All around her people staggered past, eyes red, clothes wrinkled from the overnight flight. Alex, on the other hand, felt surprisingly well-rested. Thank goodness she'd packed a washcloth and a clean top in her overnight bag, and had freshened up just before the fasten seat belts sign came on. She was refreshed, she had slept, and she was ready for anything.

She glanced at her phone, not surprised to see every notification symbol jostling for space at the top. There was always a crisis somewhere. Which for her was a good thing; promotional PR paid the bills, but it was managing the unexpected and spinning disaster into gold where she excelled.

She dialled up voicemail and waited for the first message to come through.

'Alex? It's me.'

Alex smiled as she heard the voice of Amber, her colleague and, more importantly, her friend. With just three words she was home. Home. A place she had stopped believing existed. After all, hadn't she trained herself not to rely on people or places?

'Hope you get this in time. What am I saying? Of course you will. There's no way you don't have a fully charged phone ready to switch on the second you land! So, we've had a last-minute booking. It's a residential stay and the client is very much demanding that you get there asap. So you need to head straight there. I've arranged for a car to pick you up and take you. Give me a call when you're on the way and I can go through everything with you. Don't worry, I packed up some clothes for you and they've been collected. Well done again on New York. You rocked it. Can't believe we're properly international! Talk soon!'

The voicemail ended and Alex frowned as

she saved it. She hadn't been expecting to head straight out again—after a week away she was more than ready to return to the Chelsea townhouse she had inherited the year before and turned into both a home and the business premises for her three closest—and only—friends. Together they had set up the Happy Ever After Agency, offering regular, one-off and consultancy support in everything from admin to events, PR to bespoke jobs.

Only eight months after opening they already had a strong reputation, backed up by glowing testimonials from previous clients. Glowing testimonials thanks to their ability to react quickly. Exactly as she needed to do right now, she reminded herself. Her feelings didn't matter. The client always came first.

Of course it didn't hurt their reputation that one of their previous clients, Prince Laurent, Archduke of Armaria, was currently courting Emilia, their events specialist, whilst tech billionaire Deangelo Santos was engaged to Harriet, his former PA and their head of admin.

Alex suppressed a sigh. They'd been open less than a year and already it was all change. Next year Harriet would marry Deangelo and officially move out of the townhouse, and they all knew Laurent would propose to Emilia any day now.

Harriet intended to carry on working once she was married but, although Emilia would remain a business partner, there was no way she would be able to take on any jobs once she became Archduchess. Alex was absolutely delighted for her friends, but she couldn't help wishing they'd had more time together first. Time to really build the agency.

She swallowed, not wanting to admit even to herself that the ache she felt deep inside wasn't just down to the changes in the business. She'd been so happy these last few months, living and working with her friends. She'd trained herself to enjoy her own company, but the house felt alive with the four of them in it. It was welcoming. Would it seem empty when there were just two?

Pushing the dark thoughts away, Alex walked swiftly through Customs, checking her emails as she did so and flicking through her clients' social media feeds to make sure there was nothing requiring immediate attention.

She was just aware enough of her surroundings to make sure she didn't crash into anyone, otherwise she zoned out the noise and hubbub as she exited into the Arrivals

Hall. She stopped for a moment, scanning the waiting crowds for a sign with her name on it, but before she could spot it her attention was snagged by a teenage girl running past her to launch herself into the arms of a middle-aged couple, whose wide smiles and bright eyes showed how very glad they were to see her.

No one had ever waited for Alex unless they'd been paid to be there, like the driver today. She watched as the couple enfolded the girl in their arms, unable to help noticing other reunions, some loud, some tearful, and one so passionate she felt like a voyeur.

She straightened. Enough of this nonsense. She had just had a very successful few days, turning the agency into an international proposition, and she was heading straight into another job. Success, security, everything she was working towards was within reach. That was where she needed to focus.

With a jolt of relief, she spotted the sign with her name on it and headed towards it. The sooner she was out of the airport the better.

Ten minutes later Alex found herself ensconced in the back of a comfortable saloon car, her laptop purring to life beside her, a notebook on the folded-out tray table, a chilled bottle of water and a pot of fruit beside it. She read through her emails again quickly, but there was nothing from Amber to indicate where she was going and what she would be doing once she was there.

The driver had volunteered the information that the journey would take around an hour and a half, depending on traffic, but hadn't mentioned the destination. No matter. Amber would fill her in.

Despite the earliness of the hour the roads were busy and the car crawled along. Looking out of the darkened windows into the pre-dawn winter gloom, Alex noted how low and heavy the skies were. The temperature had dropped as well, now closer to the New York chill she'd just left than the autumnal mildness she'd flown away from just a week ago.

It was easy to believe that Christmas was less than three weeks away and winter was well and truly settling in.

A sign caught her eye and she winced at the realisation that they were heading out to the M40. Hopefully they'd turn off soon. She normally avoided the area around the Chilterns. It was far too full of memories.

She checked her phone and decided that it was late enough to call Amber. Barely had she pressed the call button when her friend answered, sounding, as always, far too chipper for first thing in the morning.

'Hi, Alex! You got my message?'

'I did. Which is why I am in the back of a car heading *out* of London and not into it. Who's the client and what's so urgent that I'm needed on site straight away? A threatened exposé? PR disaster?' Her mind whirled. The thornier the problem the more she loved it.

'Nothing so exciting. I'm sorry. But hopefully you'll still enjoy the brief. Have you heard of Hawk?'

Alex thought for a moment, the name niggling at her. 'It sounds familiar.'

'It's an outdoor lifestyle brand, all rugged clothing, popular with those people who like to leave their city pad in their four-by-four to go for a ten-minute walk on the beach, but the clothes are the real deal as well, you know? They're worn by loads of serious climbers and explorer types. They have that cute hawk symbol on all their clothes. Like my winter coat?'

'Yes. I know who you mean.' She didn't own any of their clothing personally, but she was aware of the company's stellar reputation. 'What's happened? Why do they need me?'

'A broken leg.'

Alex blinked. Maybe she wasn't as refreshed as she thought. 'A broken leg?'

'Their PR manager has managed to break her leg in several places. She's confined to bed with her leg in a cage.'

That made more sense. 'I see.'

'They've just moved their headquarters to some kind of stately home out towards Swindon, I think. That's where you're headed.'

Alex let out a breath she hadn't quite realised she was holding. Swindon was past the danger area. 'Okay…'

'The owner is opening up the whole estate as an outdoor activity and nature destination. You know the kind of thing: adventure playgrounds and forest trails, all in line with the whole Hawk brand. They're running the business out of converted barns, or stables, or something suitably rustic. They're officially opening at the end of the week, with a ton of Christmas-themed events. Apparently the house and grounds were all neglected and it's the kind of area where jobs are sparse, house prices sky-high and lots of incomers are buying second homes, so there's a whole rejuvenating-the-village and local-jobs-for-local-people thing going on as well.'

'Very worthy,' Alex said drily. 'But any Communications and PR plan for all that will have been agreed months ago. What do they need me for?'

'To look after things while the PR manager is on bed-rest.'

Alex shifted, staring out of the window at the pinkening sky. 'Amber, that's not a difficult job. Any of our temps could take a plan and implement it. They don't need me for anything so simple. It's not like I'm cheap.'

'They were adamant they wanted you. It's a big deal, Alex. Opening up the house after all this time is a huge undertaking, and it's very different to anything they've done before. They see the estate as the embodiment of their brand. They're really big on sustainability and corporate responsibility, which fits in with the job creation and community stuff. They need a safe pair of hands to make sure it's properly publicised. Besides, they hinted that there might be bigger work coming our way if they were happy. Maybe this is some kind of test.'

'Maybe…' But Alex had entered PR for a reason. She knew when someone was spinning a story and this situation just didn't ring true. 'Send me the brief, will you?'

'I don't have it. They wanted to talk you through it all in person. But, honestly, they are opening with a whole Christmassy bang. You'll be kept suitably busy, I promise.'

All Alex's senses tingled. As soon as she finished the call she planned to find out every last bit of knowledge she could about Hawk and its owner. If it was in the public domain—or semi-public—then she would find it. Maybe she was wrong, and this situation was all absolutely legitimate, but she needed to be prepared for any and every eventuality.

'Alex, before you go… Dalstone sent over their press release for you to work your magic on and they want it back before nine this morning. Can you take a look now?'

'Of course. I'll send it right back. Is everything else okay?'

'All's good. Harriet's working from home today. Deangelo just got back from an oversea trip so she wants to see him. Emilia's event went really well, but she didn't get in until after two so I think she'll be sleeping in.'

Amber sounded wistful. She thrived on the company of others and was happiest when they were all together. It didn't help that Christmas was so close. For the last few years the four of them had spent Christmas together, but this year Deangelo was taking Harriet back to his native Rio De Janeiro for the holiday, and Emilia would be spending two weeks in Armaria. All three of them expected their friend to come back sporting an engagement ring.

'I was thinking,' Alex said with an impulsiveness that surprised her. 'You and I should do something this Christmas. Skiing, maybe? Or we could have a city break somewhere wintry, like Vienna?'

'Really?'

'Absolutely. Why don't you look into it? After all the hard work we've had over the last few months we deserve a short break.'

'It will have to be short,' Amber reminded her. 'Your contract with Hawk lasts until Christmas Eve, and we have the Van Daemon New Year's Eve charity ball, but we could do three days in between without any problems.'

'Three days sounds perfect. Okay, I'll get the press release straight back. Speak later.'

'Give me a call when you're fully briefed and settled in. I'm sorry you had to head out on another job without coming home first.'

'It's fine. It's what we're here to do. It's a good sign, Amber. A sign we're where we want to be.'

Alex finished the call and opened her laptop, connecting it to her phone's data so she could access the press release Amber had mentioned. And then, she reminded herself, it would be time to investigate her new employers and check just why her every hackle was up and sensing danger.

But the press release needed far more work than she had anticipated, and between the pull of her work and the lull induced by the car's steady process she soon got lost in it, any thought of research flying out of her head.

She didn't notice the car turn off the motorway long before Swindon, and nor was she aware as they drove through a succession of idyllic villages, more like a film set than real places, with a succession of village greens, quirky pubs and thatched cottages.

It wasn't until the car slowed and turned in at a pair of elaborate gates that she realised she'd arrived at her destination.

'Already?' she muttered, glancing at the time on her laptop.

Only an hour had passed. There was no way they had made it to Swindon in that time. Which meant they were somewhere else entirely; somewhere an hour west of London. Inhaling slowly, Alex looked up. There was no need to worry. She was in control; she was always in control.

Repeating the mantra, she looked straight ahead at the gates, taking in every detail of the ornate gilt-covered iron, the curlicues and symbols, time stilling as she noted every familiar detail. Her breath caught painfully in her throat, and her mouth was dry as the old, unwelcome panic, banished for a decade, thundered through her.

She hadn't just arrived. She'd returned. She was at Blakeley. Ten years after swearing never to set foot here again. Ten years after renouncing her way of life and starting anew.

Calm deserted her. She couldn't do this. Wouldn't. The car would have to turn around and take her straight back to London.

Hands shaking, she began to bundle her phone back into her bag, snapping her laptop shut. But she couldn't find the words to tell the driver to stop. Her chest was too tight, her throat swollen with fear and long-buried memories.

And still the car purred inexorably on. Every curve of the drive, every tree and view was familiar. More. It was part of her soul. Alex sat transfixed, fear giving way to nostalgic wonder, and for a moment she saw the ghost of a fearless long-limbed girl flitting through the trees.

But that girl was long gone. Lady Lola Beaumont had disappeared the day the Beaumonts' fortunes had crashed and in her place

Alexandra Davenport had appeared. Any resemblance was purely superficial.

Besides, who would recognise flamboyant Lola in demure Alex? Alexandra didn't party or flirt, she didn't dance through life expecting favours to be bestowed upon her, and she didn't try to shock or crave publicity. She worked hard; she lived a quiet existence. Her clothes were fashionable and stylish, yes, but on the sensible side. Her hair was coiled neatly, her jewellery discreet. And it was Alexandra Davenport who had been employed to do a job. The fact that the job was at her old family home must be one awful coincidence.

It *had* to be. After all, no one knew who she once had been. Not even her best friends.

Alex sat frozen, still undecided. Turning tail and running wasn't her style, but she had stayed clear of this entire region for a reason. She might not feel like Lola any longer, might not act like her, but what if someone recognised her?

Her hands folded into fists. She managed the story; she was no longer the story herself. She'd left her tabloid headline existence in the past, where it belonged, but she knew her reappearance at her childhood home would create nothing but speculation and the kind of publicity she'd spent a decade avoiding.

If she turned around now she wouldn't be running away, she'd be making a prudent retreat. She could claim a double booking and send one of her many capable temps in her stead, with a discreet discount and an apology. It was the right—the only—thing to do.

Only at that moment the car swept round the last bend and there it was, gleaming gold in the winter morning sun. Blakeley Castle. Alex could only stare transfixed at the long, grand façade, at the famous turrets, the formal gardens, now autumnal in browns and oranges and red, the trees bare of leaves, their spindly branches reaching high to the grey-blue sky. Her breath quickened and she leaned forward as if in a trance.

Blakeley Castle was beautiful. There was nowhere like it. Nowhere as steeped in myth and legend and history. Kings had fallen in love within its walls; queens had fallen from favour. Dukes had lost their hearts, and sometimes their heads, and the Beaumonts had gambled their fortunes, their titles, their freedom, their looks and their marriages on games of chance, of love, of treason.

Until one had gambled too much and lost it all. His freedom, his family, his home.

And now his daughter, the last Beaumont, was returning to Blakeley. But as an anonymous employee, no longer the spoiled darling of the house.

Alex took a deep breath, straightening her shoulders. She might have changed her name and changed her destiny but the old ancestral cry of 'Semper porsum', always forward, ran through her veins. This was just a job. And Blakeley was just a house—well, a castle. But it was still bricks and mortar. There were no ghosts here apart from the few that still haunted her dreams. And she made sure they vanished in the cold light of day.

She wasn't Lola Beaumont. She was Alexandra Davenport. She was calm and capable and she always saw her commitments through. Her life was sensible and measured and it was ridiculous to think of upsetting any aspect of it because of an old link to a mere place. A link that had been severed ten years ago. Nobody here knew her. She would do her job to the best of her ability and leave without looking back once. No regrets. She'd had too many of them.

Mind made up, Alex sat back as the car swept into the parking area at the side of the house, checking herself in her mirror. Her lipstick was in place, her hair neat, her expression coolly inscrutable. All was as it should be. The panic had gone. It was back in the past where it belonged. Nothing fazed her, nothing touched her, and her walls were firmly back in place.

She couldn't help noticing the changes in the familiar. Everything looked better cared for, and the flag flying from the highest turret bore a bird of prey, not the Beaumont crest. The car park was freshly laid, not a pothole to be seen, shielded from the castle by a tall hedge. She glimpsed the grand front entrance as the car turned. Doors stood open, the old faded steps were now gleaming, and the rug half covering them sported the same golden bird as that flying overhead on the flag.

Alexandra Davenport had never been to Blakeley Castle before. She would wait for the driver to open the door and then look around her in curiosity as she exited the car, asking if she should go in through the back door or report somewhere else. All would be unfamiliar, all new. She would be focussed on the task ahead. The beauty of the old house and grounds were of secondary importance, and her curiosity about the new owners confined to a moment's idle speculation before work took over, as it always did.

One deep breath and any dangerous traces of Lola disappeared as Alexandra stepped out of the car, her expression bland, her smile practised, and turned to face the person who had appeared to greet her.

The smile only wavered for one infinitesimal second as she took in the tall, broad-shouldered man, his dark jacket and jeans showcasing lean, powerful muscles, his hair swept back off his face, dark eyes as cold as the December air.

'Hello.' Her voice stayed calm and in control as she held out a hand. 'Alexandra Davenport.'

The man's gaze only grew more sardonic as he took her hand in his. His clasp was strong, almost too strong, as if he had something to prove.

'Finn Hawkin. But you knew that. Didn't you, Lola?'

CHAPTER TWO

FINN LOOSENED HIS grip and Alex withdrew her hand from his in a smooth gesture.

'I go by Alexandra now.'

'I know. Alexandra Davenport, I believe? Of course Alexandra *is* your middle name.'

He noted her slight blink of acknowledgement with satisfaction. Maybe she wasn't quite as calm as she seemed. 'Where's the Davenport from?'

'My grandmother's maiden name.' She stepped back and looked around before her cool gaze rested on him once again, understanding in her grey eyes. 'Hawkin...hawk. Of course. I see. You always did say you'd earn enough to own somewhere like Blakeley some day. I didn't think you actually meant Blakeley itself, but that wasn't the first time I underestimated you. Congratulations, Finn, you've obviously done very well.'

Finn had been rehearsing this meeting for

the last few hours. Ever since he'd heard about his Head of PR, Penelope, having an accident. No, longer than that. Since the summer, when he had glimpsed Lola across the ballroom floor and done some digging into the agency which had organised the Armarian Midsummer Ball and its four founders. From the moment he'd realised that Alexandra Davenport was exactly who he thought she was.

Lola Beaumont was unfinished business. Business he needed to resolve in order to move on once and for all—especially now that he was master of Blakeley and all that entailed. He had to focus on the future, on his nieces, and let go all the regrets that still haunted him. And he could only do that by confronting the past—and the woman who dominated it.

And then the fates had aligned, for good or for ill, and he had taken advantage of them. Penelope's accident was more than unfortunate, coming at such a very crucial time. The castle would be opening to the public for the first time in its history this weekend, and he needed an experienced pair of hands to manage all the resulting publicity. Who better than the woman who had grown up here? Who now worked as a PR consultant?

The Lola he'd known would have reacted

to her homecoming in some dramatic fashion, with tears or laughter equally likely, but this new version radiated a disconcerting cool calmness. A calmness he hadn't anticipated, hadn't prepared for. Nor had he missed her slight emphasis on the words 'underestimated'.

His mouth tightened. He didn't reply, not at first, taking a moment to observe the woman who had been his oldest friend—and his first love.

'You didn't know I founded Hawk?'

He didn't hide his polite disbelief. Maybe she'd walked away and never so much as typed his name into a search engine or on a social media site, but his business was a global brand, and as founder and CEO he had been extensively profiled.

Alex was a PR professional. It didn't seem possible that she had no idea of who he had become and what he'd achieved.

But her smile was apologetic. 'Sorry. Outdoor pursuits aren't my speciality and nor is clothing. I'm aware of Hawk, of course, but you've never been a rival of any of my clients, so I haven't ever needed to investigate further. That was why I was so surprised when Amber said you had requested me specifically. I have to say I am even more surprised now I'm here. Finn, obviously it's flattering that you would like me to cover your PR. But, given everything, I don't think that our working together is in any way a good idea.'

'Everything?' He kept his voice icily smooth, but she still didn't react, her expression unruffled.

'Our shared history.'

He raised an eyebrow. 'Shared history? That's one way of putting it, I suppose.'

He stopped himself from saying anything else, from letting the bitter words he'd been holding back for ten years come spilling out. He was no longer a young man with no idea how to handle his emotions, how to cope with accusations and betrayal and heartbreak.

'However, that's exactly why you're perfect for this job. After all, you know the castle better than anyone else.'

Again, just a blink as her reaction. Finn folded his arms and waited for her to respond, refusing to allow her calmness to throw him. After all, whether she called herself Alexandra Davenport or Lola Beaumont, there was one thing he knew for sure: she didn't just know Blakeley Castle, she loved it with every fibre of her fiery being.

But, he conceded as he studied her, this

woman wasn't fiery. Gone was the platinum blonde hair and dramatic eyeliner, the cutting-edge fashion and almost fey wildness. Instead Alexandra's hair was her natural light brown, neatly pinned up, her make-up discreet, her clothes professional. There was nothing wild in the way she stood, nor in her eyes. Instead Finn noted her absolute air of control. Was there any trace of Lola trapped inside this stranger?

'The castle, yes. Your brand, no.'

'But you specialise in short-term jobs, in getting up to speed quickly,' he pointed out silkily. 'I have a whole team who can manage Hawk's PR work. What I need is someone to help me launch Blakeley Castle as a destination. Your expertise and knowledge make you the logical choice. Your colleague, Amber, didn't think there would be any problem.'

'Amber doesn't know that I have any personal connection to Blakeley—or to you,' she added in a low voice. 'So of course she wouldn't foresee any conflict of interest. But there are conflicts, and it's my professional opinion that you would be better off with one of our excellent consultants instead of me. I can think of at least three who would be perfect. I propose I go back to London now and send you their profiles. I can make sure your preferred candidate is with you by the end of the day. I'm sorry you have wasted your time. It's unfortunate that I was out of contact when you called.'

She picked up her bag and took a decisive step back.

'I'm glad to see you've done so well, Finn. I look forward to our companies working together. I'm sure it will be a successful partnership.'

Not so fast. He hadn't got her back just to watch her drive off into the sunset with nothing resolved.

'You've signed a contract.'

Her eyes flickered. 'And we'll honour that contract…'

'The contract specifies you, Alex. That *you* will work here at Blakeley Castle until Christmas Eve. Not one of your consultants, however excellent they may be.'

'Yes, but —'

'It's you I have employed, your expertise I want, and your exorbitant rates I have agreed to.'

'We can, of course, offer a discount to offset any inconvenience.'

'I don't need a discount. Either you fulfil the terms of your contract or I sue you for breaking them. Your choice. I'm sure you'll

be happy to stand up in court and tell everyone why you didn't feel able to work for me.'

Her silence and stillness were absolute. 'I
see. I'm sorry that you hate me this much,
Finn...'

'I don't hate you, Lola. I have absolutely
no feelings at all towards you. This isn't personal. This is business. So what will it be?'

He held her gaze, conscious of the lie. Of
course it was personal, but his business reasons were more than valid. And he didn't hate
her. He never had.

She sighed. 'If you're absolutely adamant
that I stay then of course I will, but I'd like to
make it clear that I think you would be better letting me assign someone else to this job.
Are you sure this is what you want?'

'I'm sure. Come along and I'll show you
to your desk. Not that you need me to show
you anywhere. I'm sure you remember your
way around.'

Her eyes dipped briefly and she laid a hand
on his arm, her touch light. Even her touch
had lost its fire. Or maybe he was immune,
their past having inoculated him against any
spells she might cast.

'Finn, I need to get one thing straight.
If you really want me to work for you then
please forget you ever knew me. Forget I ever

lived here. Lola Beaumont is gone. I left her behind a long time ago.'

'Shame. There was a lot of good in Lola behind it all.'

'That's neither here nor there. Do I have your word that you will respect my anonymity? The reputation I have built up? I don't know how you tracked me down, Finn, but if you really have brought me here to do my best for your business and not to create a whole other kind of publicity then you'll forget about Lola.'

She fixed her disconcerting gaze on him. Still no trace of visible emotion in their grey depths. No longer could a lovestruck boy compare them to stormy seas or windswept skies. Instead they were more like a glossy pebble, smooth and unreadable.

'Unless, of course, it's other publicity that you are after? Not my expertise but my past?'

Finn stared at her, incredulous as her meaning took shape. 'You think I brought you here to expose you?'

She shrugged. 'It would be excellent PR. The last Beaumont back at Blakeley. . The papers would love it. They'll rake up the old scandal anyway, you know that—you must be counting on it. Everyone loves the idea of an old, proud family brought down, and now they can stand on the spot where it happened. I am quite happy to facilitate that, Finn, but I am no longer personally part of that story.'

His hands curled once more into fists as he fought to match her calmness. 'I don't expect you to be the story. Blakeley is mine now. I prefer to concentrate on the future and on building prosperity for everyone who works here.'

'Thank you. I'm glad we understand each other.'

Even with the toned-down make-up and hair, the professional clothes, he could still see traces of the vibrant girl he had known in the tilt of Alexandra's pointed chin, the curve of her cheekbones, her elegant posture. But any resemblance was purely skin-deep.

Lola was gone, and with her all that fire and passion. It might have got her—and all who knew her—into trouble sometimes, but she had at least known how to live. He got the impression that the woman in front of him didn't really live a single day of her ordered life. Rather she sleepwalked through it, merely existing. Of all the tragedies that had hit the Beaumonts, this seemed like the biggest tragedy of all.

But whether she called herself Alexandra or Lola one thing was clear—she still thought he would use her, expose her for his own personal gain, just as she had believed ten years ago. No matter what he had achieved, to the woman opposite he was still the boy she thought had betrayed her. Well, his word might not have been good enough then, but she would have to believe in it now.

His future awaited him, and once Christmas was over Lola/Alexandra would be out of his life and his memories for good.

Control had been at the centre of Alex's life for many years now, but she had never had to fight so hard for it as she did right now. Standing beside her old home, with its turrets reaching up into the skies, standing opposite the man she had once given her whole heart and trust to, only for him to rip them— and her—to pieces, had whipped up feelings and emotions she had long thought buried and gone. Nausea swirled through her and her hands shook, but she fought to keep her voice even and her expression bland.

Finn could never know the effect he had on her. She would never give him— or anyone—that kind of power again.

'I think I'd better get started. Where shall I set up? I would usually arrive fully prepared, but I was told I'd be briefed when I got here.'

She allowed the merest hint of accusation to hang in the air. Finn had deliberately allowed her to turn up unprepared and wrong-footed. Although, she allowed, if she hadn't been too absorbed in her work to do the background check she'd promised herself, then she wouldn't have been quite so unprepared. She couldn't blame Finn for everything. Not this time.

'I'll take you to meet your team and brief you on the way. Leave your bags. One of the staff will take them to your rooms. The Hawk offices are in the stables. This way.'

Finn indicated the freshly laid woodchip path which wound away from the car park into the small copse which separated the newly refurbished offices from the castle. Alexandra hefted her leather laptop bag onto her shoulder and followed him—as if she didn't know the way to the stables just as well as he did.

'Amber said you're planning to open the castle up to the public and the launch is this week—is that right?' She barely waited for his nod before continuing. 'So, will you open all year round or just for Christmas? Seasonally? Weekends? What about the gardens? Will they have different opening hours and prices? Obviously I should have researched this before I started, but I only got off my flight a couple of hours ago.'

Every question was direct and to the point. Information-gathering for her job, no more. She had to treat this like any other job, Finn like any other client. It was the only way she was going to get through this.

'My apartments are in the top two floors of the west wing, and private, but the rest of the castle, including the grounds, will be open every day. Houses like this should be for everyone, not just for the privileged few.'

Alex swallowed, tightening her hold on her bag. Finn was living in her home, her beloved castle. Once she had daydreamed of such a situation, only in her dreams she had been living there alongside him. Was there a woman living with him? He wasn't wearing a wedding ring but that didn't mean anything. Not that she cared. She just hoped he'd learnt loyalty in the last decade. How to love, not how to use.

Although, judging by the way he was using her right now, she wouldn't bet on it.

'I assume all the paintings and furniture are still here? I know the castle was bought complete.'

She fought to suppress a dangerously revealing wobble in her voice. This was a job, not personal. Blakeley and all its treasures meant nothing to her. She couldn't think about the old oak furniture that dated back to Tudor times, or the famous collection of Pre-Raphaelite paintings. She couldn't remember the old dolls' house or Strawberry, her beloved pony.

Finn nodded. 'Luckily for me the castle was bought by an oligarch who never actually visited the place. Rumour in the village is that he wanted a hunting lodge and didn't realise the estate wasn't suitable for the kind of stag-hunting he'd planned. I don't think he even set foot in the place. Blakeley hadn't been touched since the day you left.'

Alex allowed herself one dangerous moment of memory. One flashback to the desperate girl with tears streaming down her face, the police tape still flickering around the lake, the hardness on Finn's face, the paparazzi pressed up against the gates. And the last look back before she had slipped out of the secret door in the wall and out of her life, leaving Lola in the headlines and her heart in Blakeley's keeping.

And then she pushed that memory firmly back down and picked up the pace. 'So, Finn,' she said as brightly as she could. 'Tell me more about your plans and what you need me to do.'

Work was the answer. Work had always been the answer. And for the next few weeks she suspected it was going to be her salvation.

CHAPTER THREE

ALEXANDRA DREW IN a deep breath and stared fixedly at her laptop screen, refusing to let the letters in front of her blur or her mind wander. She was focussed and busy, just the way she liked it, with all messy emotions kept at bay.

All around was a low hum of activity: the sound of a contented, productive office. Sitting here, it was hard to imagine that this building had once been ramshackle stables. There wasn't a whiff of straw or old leather to be found. When she'd first walked in she'd passed the place where her old mare, Strawberry, had been stabled, and for one terrifying moment had been catapulted back in time. Luckily, the receptionist had spoken to her and pulled her back to the present.

She didn't want to go back. She couldn't…

No, better to focus on the present. And if she concentrated hard she could do exactly that.

It helped that the once familiar room was

now so unfamiliar. The architect had done an amazing job of transforming the dark old buildings into a light, airy and modern space. On the ground floor was a spacious reception area, meeting rooms, and what Finn had described as 'creative space', filled with sofas, board games and a kitchen area.

The executive offices were also housed on the bottom floor, but she hadn't been shown them. Instead Finn had taken her upstairs to the general offices, making it very clear what her position was.

Upstairs was one big office area, with pale wood desks blending in with old oiled beams, the walls matt white, the floor gleaming parquet, and wide windows showcasing breathtaking views of the parkland and estate gardens.

Alexandra had barely given them a glance. There was a reason she'd moved to London. Not only did she prefer the anonymity of the city, she also liked the way the noise and hub-bub gave her so little space to think. London was overwhelming, and that was exactly how she liked it. There was no space to be an individual. The city assimilated you and you just had to be swept away.

Finn had introduced her to the team and his marketing director before leaving her with a curt nod. For a moment, watching him stride away, she had almost felt lost. She'd swiftly shaken that absurdity from her mind, but now, as she read through her handover notes and began to get to grips with her workload, it began to dawn on Alex just what Finn had achieved. Her childhood playmate, her first crush, the boy she had naively thought she might love, had achieved his dream.

She tapped a pencil absentmindedly on the desk as she looked around at the comfortable space filled with people hard at work. He had always proclaimed that one day he would travel around the world, that he'd own his own company and make a fortune, and live in a place like Blakeley, not just work there. And she'd believed him, that fierce determined, skinny boy with his messy dark brown hair and chocolate eyes. Even though he'd never even travelled as far as Oxford, and his father and grandfather and every generation before them had been born, had worked and died within the castle grounds.

But for a while it had looked as if his dreams had stagnated—a pregnant sister, an alcoholic father demanding all his time and attention. The boy who had dreamt of the world had found himself bound to one place, and meanwhile her burgeoning modelling career had taken her around the globe. How he must have resented it. Resented her.

The pencil stilled and the old questions once more flooded her mind. Was that why he had done it? Betrayed her when she had already been as down as a girl could be? The money from those photos must have freed him. And look what he had achieved with that freedom. Did he ever consider that he'd purchased it with her innocence and happiness? Or did he think that it was a fair trade for the generations of Hawkins who had been trampled on by generations of Beaumonts?

Another inhale. Another exhale. Push it all away. All those inconvenient feelings. Concentrate on the job in front of you.

She'd been Alex for so long there were times when she forgot that Lola had even existed. She needed that blissful ignorance now. She had to treat this as any other job, forget she knew Finn, not allow herself to speculate on how he'd found her and why he had gone to such trouble to bring her here. Forget everything but the task at hand.

She put the pencil down firmly, pulling her laptop closer, and as she did so a pretty darkhaired girl approached her desk.

'Hi, is it Alex or Alexandra?'

'I answer to both.' She smiled in welcome

as she desperately searched her mind for the girl's name. Katy? Kitty?

'I'm Kaitlin.' The girl smiled shyly back. 'I doubt you'll remember anyone after that quick introduction. I've never known Finn to be in such a hurry. I thought you might want to get settled in today, but I'll make sure you get properly introduced to everyone tomorrow, so you know what they actually do. I'm the PR Assistant, so technically I report to you. I suggest you ask me anything you need to know and I'll do my best to point you in the right direction.'

Kaitlin's friendliness was disarming—and a relief after the frosty civility Finn had shown. 'That's good to know. Nice to meet you properly, Kaitlin.'

'Penelope asked me to talk you through her strategy and plans so you can go to her with any questions before things get too manic. Is now good?'

'Now's great, thanks.'

Alex looked at her neat notes, perfectly aligned, finding the long to-do list its usual balm. At first she had been at a loss as to why she was so urgently required. Penelope, Hawk's laid-up Head of PR was organised and had clearly taught her junior staff well. Looking through her notes, strategies and task lists, Alex saw that it appeared that there was little left for Alex to actually do, apart from follow instructions. A job anyone with half a brain could manage. It didn't seem worth her substantial fee, and her lurking suspicion that Finn had tracked her down and employed her simply to gloat about their reversal of fortune had deepened.

But as she read on it became clear that the plan Penelope had put together would need careful tweaks and adjustments as the castle was finally opened to the public, and the potential press interest needed to be handled by someone with experience. It was a job she was confident any of the temps on her books could handle, but she could see that Finn genuinely needed outside help, and as it was unlikely he'd manufactured Penelope's accident her presence here was in some way coincidental, even if her concern as to how he had tracked her down remained.

After all, if he could then so could any of those journalists who still ran occasional stories on the fall of the Beaumonts.

Kaitlin pulled a chair up to the desk. 'So, the first thing is the media launch party. May I…?'

Alex nodded permission and the younger woman manipulated the mouse on the PC

Alex had been allocated and brought up the appropriate file.

'Here are the notes and the event plan. It's on Thursday night, and the party is for journalists, local dignitaries and VIPs. The castle will then have a soft opening for two weeks and will officially celebrate with a second, bigger party on the twenty-fourth of December. That party will include locals, colleagues, suppliers, partners…everyone, really.'

Alex inhaled as she read the timeline.

The official opening of the castle and grounds will be marked with a traditional Christmas Eve party.

'Christmas Eve?' Somehow she kept her voice calm.

'Apparently it's a real tradition at Blakeley. I hear the parties here used to be wild. Full of every kind of celebrity from pop stars to princes.'

'Right. Then we need to make sure we publicise that angle.'

Her heart began to thump; her hands felt damp. Christmas Eve. Her birthday. More than that, the day Blakeley had always celebrated Christmas.

For generations, friends and lovers, enemies and rivals had descended on Blakeley on Christmas Eve to feast and dance, intrigue and plot.

As a child Alex would spend the afternoon hosting a sumptuously over-the-top party for her friends—and then spend the evening darting through the dancing, flirting adults, sipping champagne from discarded glasses and sneaking canapés. No one had ever told her to go to bed. Instead she had been the spoilt princess of the house, petted and indulged, falling asleep on a chair or a sofa, where she would wake on Christmas morning to find herself covered with some discarded jacket.

In her mid-teens the two parties had been combined, with lithe, knowing teenagers far too at home amidst the glamour and heady atmosphere of the adult affair. At least they'd pretended they were at home. Alex had been very good at pretending. Until the night of her eighteenth birthday, that was, when her world had become real for the first time—for a few blissful hours, until the moment when it had stilled and stopped for ever.

She tried to inhale again, to take those sweet, calming breaths that kept her pulse even, her heart still, her head clear. But her breath caught in her throat.

I can't do this, she thought, panic threatening to flood through the walls she had built so carefully, so painstakingly, solid walls, covered in ivy and thorns, ready to repel all invaders. *I can't.*

But she could. She had no choice. Stay and deal with it or leave and run the risk of exposure.

She was stronger than this. Nothing and no one could hurt her now. Blakeley was just a place, Christmas Eve was just a date, her birthday would go unremarked. She would show Finn that he hadn't won. Not then, not now. And she would do so by making sure his planned launch ran absolutely perfectly.

Gradually her pulse returned to normal, her emotions stilled, and she calmly made another note.

Check the invite list for the Christmas party.

'Okay,' she said, her voice as steady as ever. 'What's next?'

The conversation with Kaitlin was illuminating in several ways, taking up the rest of the morning and lunch. It had been a long time since her airline breakfast, and Alex had had no chance to get anything to eat, but Kaitlin ordered a working lunch, which the two ate at the desk as they finished going through the notes. Alex's to-do list was getting satisfactorily ever longer.

At some point in the afternoon the younger woman finally returned to her own desk and Alex sank thankfully into work. There she could forget that Christmas Eve had once meant something, meant everything, deep in the absorption that working out how to craft and manipulate a story gave her.

As always, she lost track of time, and when she finally stretched and looked up she realised it was now dark outside, the office lights bright against the gloom. The room was almost deserted. Just a few people were left at their desks and they seemed to be packing up. Alex leaned back and stretched again, glad that the weeks ahead looked interesting but achievable.

She would give Finn no reason, no excuse to find fault with a single thing she did. He had the power and the influence now. With one word he could tell everyone who she was—who she'd used to be—and trash her fledgling agency's reputation. She wouldn't have thought him capable once. She knew better now.

'Alex?' Kaitlin hovered by her desk, her

bag already on her shoulder. 'I'm off now. Is there anything you need before I leave?'

'No, I'm fine. Thank you. You've been so helpful.'

'I hope so.' The younger woman looked pleased, brushing her thick dark hair away from her face as her cheeks turned a little pink.

Alex looked around at the gleaming new office. 'I guess you haven't been based here very long?'

'No, Finn's been here since the summer, but the rest of us moved in October. There's still a London office, but the plan is to scale it right back. For now some people are splitting their time between there and here. It's easier for those of us without families, I guess. Finn has converted an old mill into flats and a few rent there. One or two rent in the village and quite a lot of us are in Reading—we're not ready for a totally rural life just yet!'

'It's impressive that so many of you were ready to uproot yourselves.'

'Finn's so inspiring...his whole ethos. I wouldn't want to be anywhere else.'

'That's reassuring to hear. I hope I'll feel the same way.'

'I hope so too.'

The deep masculine tones made both Alex

and Kaitlin jump, the latter's cheeks going even redder as Finn sauntered towards them.

'Loyalty is very important here at Hawk.'

But it wasn't Finn's unexpected appearance that made Alex's pulse speed up, and nor was it the sardonic gleam in his eye as he looked at her. It was the two small girls holding on to his hands. Finn had *children*? He had security, money, her old home and a family? Everything she had lost. Everything she would never have.

The oldest girl looked, to Alex's inexperienced eye, to be about nine, the other around five. They were both in school uniform, their dark hair so like Finn's own in messy plaits, and the same dark, dark eyes fixed on Alex.

'It's the Sleeping Princess,' the younger one said, pointing at Alex. 'Look, Saffy, it's the Princess from the painting.'

Finn suppressed a grin as Alexandra's startled gaze flew to his. Turned out the lady could show surprise after all.

'Alex…' The name felt clumsy on his tongue. 'I'd like you to meet my nieces. Saffron, Scarlett, this is Alex. She's working here for a little while.'

'No, Uncle Finn.' Scarlett tugged at his hand. 'She's a princess in disguise.'

Wasn't that the truth?

'Nice to meet you.' Alex smiled uncertainly at the girls. 'But I'm afraid it's a case of mistaken identity. I'm not a princess, although it's lovely to be thought one.'

'You *are*,' Scarlett insisted.

Kaitlin nodded. 'I see what you mean, Scarlett. You're thinking of that painting, aren't you? The one of Blakeley Castle and the Sleeping Beauty? She does look a little like Alex.'

Alex's cheeks reddened, just slightly. Finn was certain she knew exactly which painting Scarlett was referring to; it was a Rossetti, part of the castle's famed Pre-Raphaelite collection. Alex's great-great-grandmother was the model: a woman who in her youth had been as scandalous as her granddaughter several times removed.

What would the Pre-Raphaelite muse and late-Victorian It Girl think of her descendant? Would she recognise this poised, apparently emotion-free woman sitting in an office chair as if she were made for it, the very model of efficiency? Finn barely recognised her himself. It was all too easy to think her who she claimed to be.

'If you say so, but I can't see it myself,' he said, taking pity on Alex, even though her resemblance to the woman in the painting had been notable when she was younger and was still remarkable, despite her decidedly un-Pre-Raphaelite appearance. 'I'll take it from here, Kaitlin.' He nodded at the dark-haired girl. 'You get off now or you'll miss the last bus.'

'Bus?' Alex watched Kaitlin leave before swivelling back to face him. 'Since when was there a bus?'

'If I want my employees to come and bury themselves in the depths of the Chilterns then I have to make it manageable for them,' Finn pointed out. 'Some live on the estate in the Old Corn Mill, but that didn't suit everyone, so a mini-bus goes between here and Reading several times a day. It picks up at the train station too. Not everyone is ready to leave London just yet. And when the employees don't use it, the villagers do.'

'How very Sir Galahad of you...riding to the rescue with your jobs and renovations and buses.'

Alex's voice and face were bland, but Finn felt the barb, hidden as it was. The situation was getting to her more than she was letting on, and he had to admit he was relieved. It didn't seem normal for anyone to be so serene when confronted with their past in the way she had been.

'The village must be very grateful.'

He shrugged. 'Relieved more than grateful. Goodness knows it needed a Sir Galahad to swoop in after the Beaumonts' reign of benign neglect, followed by a decade of an indifferent and absent landlord.'

His barb wasn't hidden at all, and he saw her flinch with some satisfaction. The Beaumonts had adored being the Lord and Lady of the Manor but they hadn't been so interested in the people who lived and worked on the estate.

Blakeley might be situated in a wealthy commuter county, but the village itself was very rural, its twisty roads and the Chiltern Hills making even a short journey as the crow flew lengthy. Plus, it was a place where more than half the houses were owned by the castle, but where the jobs that had used to come with the houses had disappeared over the years.

Picturesque as Blakeley village was, not everyone wanted to rent a home where the colour of their front door and guttering was prescribed by the estate, public transport was non-existent and the nearest town a long, windy ten miles away.

'The locals are just happy to see new life breathed into the place, and enough staff are renting to make the local businesses and the school viable. My village is breathing again.'

'*Your* village? You wear Lord of the Manor pretty well.'

Another barb. Interesting.

Finn didn't react, simply nodded towards the door. 'Are you done here? The girls are ready for their dinner and I need to show you where you're staying.'

'There's a lot to do, but I can work in my room.' Alex folded her laptop closed and slipped it into its case. 'Look, if there's a bus to the train station I might as well go back to London. The train's only half an hour or so, right? Save you the problem of putting me up.'

'It's no problem. Besides, it's not just the train. You need to factor in the half-hour journey to Reading—and that's assuming you haven't missed the bus, which you have. Then say another fifteen minutes through traffic to get to the train station. Half an hour to Paddington and then your journey at the other end. You'd rather endure a four-hour return journey than stay here?'

Her gaze flickered away. 'I don't want to put anyone out.'

She didn't want to spend the night surrounded by her past, no doubt.

'You're needed evenings and weekends until Christmas. The contract says we expect you to be on site and that's exactly where you'll be. Unless you still want to walk away.'

He allowed the hint of a threat to linger in his voice, hiding the doubt he'd spent the afternoon trying to dispel. Would it be better, after all, to take her advice and let her choose a consultant to come and work here? She could still advise from London. He'd wanted her here to resolve the past, but this woman wasn't Lola. She was a stranger.

Finn hardened his heart. He needed to give his nieces a place where they belonged, the security they hadn't had until now. He'd earnt a fortune, but a lot of his profits were ploughed back into the company and the foundation he'd set up. For the reopening of Blakeley he needed the best. And everyone agreed that Alexandra Davenport *was* the best. Her expertise and inside knowledge of the castle and estate meant she was exactly what he needed—whether she liked it or not.

Alex stood up decisively. 'I never walk away from a job, Finn, not until the client is happy. I'm fine staying here if that's what you want. Whatever's easiest. You're the client.'

Finn rubbed his chin, feeling the rasp of stubble under his fingertips, suddenly weary. 'Come on, then,' he said brusquely. 'I'll show you where you're staying.'

He rounded up the girls and made his way down the stairs, all too aware of Alex following behind, the tapping of her heels on the wooden treads. He'd called the last of the Beaumonts home to Blakeley. It was up to him to control the situation. He was the boss now, and the sooner Alex accepted that, the better.

CHAPTER FOUR

NEITHER SPOKE AS Finn led Alexandra out of the stable and onto the dimly lit path. The castle reared up, lit up against the winter dark sky, and he noticed Alex turn away from it. So she wasn't as impervious to coming home as she seemed. The girls skipped ahead, oblivious to the chilly atmosphere, which was colder than the rapidly lowering evening temperature.

'Do you think it might snow?' Alex said, looking up at the clouds overhead.

'It's early yet.'

'But it has snowed this early. Remember that year—' She broke off, sentence unfinished.

But he did remember. Snowball fights and sledging, hot chocolate in the kitchen and the skiing lesson she'd given him. They'd been children, no older than Saffy, still mesmerised by the wonder of snow.

A minute went by before Alex made another attempt to break the increasingly charged silence. 'Kaitlin mentioned that you'd converted the old Corn Mill into apartments. Is that where I'm staying? Or does the village pub still have rooms?'

'Yes, no and yes.'

Now it came to it, Finn felt profoundly uncomfortable. His decision on where to house her had seemed purely pragmatic at the time. Now he wasn't so sure that his thinking had been as rational as he'd told himself, with every step provoking memories.

'The Corn Mill doesn't have any space, but it isn't the only building we've renovated. For instance, we've turned the barns at the bottom of the estate into bunkhouses. Places where inner city school kids can come so they can get a chance at the outdoor life. Hiking in the Chilterns, orienteering around the estate, building shelters, that kind of thing.'

Her mouth quirked into a half-smile. A real half-smile, like the girl he'd used to know had had, and his pulse jumped at the sight.

'You're putting me in a bunkhouse?'

'No, that's just an example. We've also renovated some of the old estate cottages for holiday lets. As you know, we'll be running outdoor activities throughout most of the year, so it made sense to give people the chance to stay here.'

'Estate cottages? Not the ones in the village? The ones in the grounds? The Lodge, I suppose, and the Dower House, and…' Her voice trailed off.

'And the Gardener's Cottage. Yes.'

'I'm sleeping in the Gardener's Cottage.' It wasn't a question.

'It's the smallest so it made sense. Four of us lived there for years, Alex. I'm sure you won't find it too much of a squeeze. And don't worry. It's been done up since you last saw it. You won't have to endure my mother's taste in wallpaper or the sofa my father used to pass out on.'

'That's not what I…' She paused and then, voice bright, said, 'It sounds very charming. I can maybe do some short videos for all the social media accounts about staying there. One weekend I'll do a full day's story— fresh eggs for breakfast in the café, a walk in the woods, that kind of thing. You're right; it makes complete sense for me to stay in a holiday cottage and I'd rattle around in the Dower House. Are the others booked yet?'

'The others?'

'The Dower House and the Lodge? I guess the Foreman's Cottage and the Blacksmith's

Cottage are also holiday lets? Because if they're not let out yet then it might be worth offering them to journalists the night of the press party. And then to some influencers in the run-up to Christmas, maybe over Christmas Eve, with invitations for the party. I know the perfect people.'

For a moment, when she had said the words 'Christmas Eve' he could have sworn her voice wobbled. Just a little.

'They are all free; letting starts in the New Year. Invite whoever you'd like. Kaitlin can put you in touch with the letting team. Girls! It's getting dark. Stay close.'

Alex shot him a quick glance and he suspected she was curious about the girls' presence. But before she had a chance to ask any questions his nieces ran back, chattering on about a rabbit Scarlett was sure she'd seen in the wood, and they hadn't exhausted the topic by the time they reached the gate to the cottage.

As they neared the gate a security light was triggered, and Alex stopped just outside the fence and stared. 'It's exactly the same,' she said softly.

Finn inhaled. From the outside nothing much had changed. His father had always kept it immaculate, even at his worst—on the surface respectable, behind the perfectly painted front door a secret drinker and despot.

'Not quite the same, I hope.'

The first sight of the house still gave Finn a sucker punch to the chest every time he walked through the gate. He'd thought buying Blakeley Castle and turning it into the place he had dreamed it could be would put some of his ghosts to rest, but sometimes they haunted him even more.

'I've put in new windows and fencing and the garden needed a lot of work.' He shot a quick look at the girls, but they were playing hopscotch on the path. 'In the end Dad stopped pretending to function—I suppose there was no one here to judge. Things were in a sorry state when I took over.'

'When did your father die?'

Alex had lowered her voice. She must have noticed he didn't want the girls to overhear. Finn couldn't help remembering just how empathic she had been, especially where his family were concerned. She was the only person living who knew the whole truth. There was a strange freedom in their conversation, in not having to watch what he said, how much he revealed.

'Two years ago. He refused to leave the

cottage, refused to let me pay for anyone to help him. Sacked the cleaners I sent, left the groceries I ordered outside to rot in the rain. He died as he lived. On his own terms and with difficulty.' He snapped his mouth closed. He'd never said those words aloud before, not to anyone.

'I'm sorry,' Alex said softly. 'How about your sister? Where is she now? The girls are hers, I suppose?'

But Finn had already said too much, shown too much—and his sister and her actions was a topic he wasn't ready to share. Not yet. Although he'd need to talk about both with Alex at some point.

'Here's a key,' he said instead. 'Your bag should be inside.'

Alex took the hint, made her voice efficient again. The moment of shared memory was gone and with it an intimacy he'd not realised he'd missed.

'Right. Is there anything I need to know about the boiler or hot water?'

'It should all be working. If not, then there's an information book in the kitchen.'

'Great. Just one more thing: is there any milk or bread in? Because I came straight from the airport and I'm not as prepared as I usually like to be.'

She looked slightly embarrassed, as if she would usually turn up at a work assignment with a week's worth of groceries on her, just in case. And maybe she would.

Finn winced. The Gardener's Cottage was the first to be completely ready. All the linen and towels were there but, because they hadn't started letting, welcome hampers were yet to be organised—and they'd only known for sure that Alex was coming late the night before. The fridge and cupboards were emptier than Mother Hubbard's.

He had meant to ask Kaitlin to sort out the basics, but once he'd seen Alex to the office he had headed out onto the estate and spent the day rebuilding a wall, not questioning why he'd felt the need for hard physical exercise. The mental note to email Kaitlin had uncharacteristically slipped right out of his mind.

'Once we're up and running we'll be leaving welcome hampers, of course, but we haven't started yet. Sorry.'

'Okay,' she pulled her phone out of her pocket. 'Look into sourcing hampers,' she said clearly, before smiling at him—a brisk, businesslike smile that reminded him just what a stranger she was now. 'Believe me, if I'm going to be inviting journalists and influencers we need highly photogenic hampers. Don't worry, I'll get on to it.'

'Right. Of course.' This efficiency was why he had employed her.

She took the key and pocketed it. 'You'd better get the girls back and fed. I'll head down to the village shop.'

Ah… 'It closes at six.'

'Or the pub…'

She bit her lip on the last word and he understood her hesitation. If she was going to be recognised anywhere it would be the pub, with its loyal clientele of locals who had known her since she was a baby. But not tonight.

'They don't serve food on a Monday night.'

'Oh.' Her smile got even brighter, but there was no warmth, no light in it. 'In that case a takeaway it is.'

Finn didn't have the heart to tell her that the only takeaways available to the village were at the weekend, when a fish and chips and pizza van set up on the green for a couple of hours.

'Look, this is my fault, so I had better fix it. Come over to the castle and I'll make you some food.'

As soon as the words were said he wanted to recall them. It was too much, too soon.

There were things to say, but not tonight, not when he was still trying to work out just who Alex was.

And she clearly felt the same way, stepping back, away from him, away from his invitation. 'You don't have to do that.'

'I do,' he said drily. 'Your only alternative is water. There's not even any tea bags in the cottage as far as I know.'

'But you cooking is too much,' she protested. 'Honestly, it's been a long day, and I have a lot to be getting on with. I can just grab some eggs and beans or something and bring them back here. I don't want to be any trouble.'

'Once,' he said, in a voice so low he didn't know if she could hear him, or if he wanted her to hear him. 'Once you said trouble was your middle name.'

She looked up at him then, eyes bright. 'I was wrong. Trouble was the family curse. That's why I avoid it whenever I can.'

Finn stared back at her. At a face at once as familiar as his dreams but also that of a stranger. The same almond-shaped grey eyes, the same high cheekbones and full mouth. The same pointed chin and high forehead and look of determination. But the spark that had made Lola so irresistible was gone, and he couldn't tell if it was extinguished entirely or just slumbering, waiting for someone to rekindle it. For one soul-aching moment he wanted to find out, to take this beautiful yet lifeless woman and kiss life back into her.

'Uncle Finn! I'm hungry!'

Now it was his turn to take a step back in denial, and the cold early winter evening breeze was a welcome wake-up call. Finn couldn't believe what had just nearly happened. Kissing Lola Beaumont or kissing Alexandra Davenport—no matter which woman she was, any personal contact was a terrible idea. After all, look what had happened last time.

Even worse, he wasn't alone. The girls were right here. Weren't they damaged enough? He had promised them, promised himself, that they would only ever have love and stability in their lives, had vowed to himself that there would be no women flitting in and out. They'd only meet a girlfriend if he was pretty damn sure she'd be permanent.

'Sorry, Scarlett.' He threw her an apologetic smile and noted with a pang the pinched look on Saffy's face. 'I was just trying to persuade Alex to eat with us, I forgot to put food in her house.'

'Yes, then you can look at the picture,' Scarlett said with a beaming grin.

But Saffron's scowl just tightened further and Finn's heart ached for the small girl. With a jolt of surprise, he noticed a look of understanding cross Alex's face as she looked at his eldest niece, her expression relaxing with compassion.

'It's been a long day, so if it's okay I will just grab some bread and milk, maybe some cheese, and bring it back here,' she said, smiling at Scarlett. 'I'll see the picture some other time, though.'

'Promise?' Scarlett asked.

Alex nodded. 'Promise.'

As he turned to walk back to the castle Alex fell behind. Finn was preoccupied with Scarlett's chatter, and it wasn't until they reached the lights surrounding the castle that, looking back, he realised Alex was making determined conversation with Saffron. The girl wasn't answering—she was always slow to warm to strangers—but her posture was less defensive and for one moment he thought he saw a slight smile on her face.

So Alex still had the old charm, when she wanted to use it, and he was absurdly grateful she was using it on his prickly niece.

And then he saw it, in the lowering of her

gaze, the slight hunch in her posture—the reason Saffron's wariness had always seemed so familiar. It *was* familiar. It was the same wariness he had seen in Alex throughout her childhood—on the rare occasions when she hadn't been performing, being the bright, glittering Beaumont girl everyone had expected her to be.

He'd have done anything to protect his nieces, no matter what, but was the reason he had stepped in so very firmly, before things could go from difficult to toxic, because he had recognised the warning signs in Saffy's eyes?

He hadn't been able to protect Lola. Not from the consequences of her parents' selfishness and not from his own family's part in her downfall, and he'd been too full of his own bitterness to reassure and help her when she'd come back demanding answers at the time. No wonder he was making damned sure that Saffy was as protected as she could be. He knew the consequences.

He'd searched for Lola for years, dreading that he'd find her struggling and alone, and equally dreading that he'd find she'd moved on in true insouciant Beaumont style, not caring about the havoc she left behind her. But now he realised with blinding clarity that all he had wanted to do was put things right. And now she was finally here he had no idea if it was possible. She had her life, and he had the girls.

Maybe it was better to leave the past where it belonged. Lola was gone and Alex was a stranger. He could finally move on.

'So, if he proposes—and he will—Emilia will be a real-live princess. Well, an archduchess, but she'll be called Princess Emilia.'

Saffron's dark eyes widened. 'And she didn't know who he was when they met? It's just like a fairy-tale.'

Alex looked up and caught Finn watching them, the rather cold expression he'd been wearing much softer. Her breath caught. He really cared about his niece. Of course he did. He had always been someone who cared deeply. Which was why she had never understood why he had done what he did—to her, of all people. How he could have exposed her so publicly, sold her for thirty pieces of silver.

The old sense of betrayal caught at her heart and she swallowed back the bitterness. She couldn't indulge. Not here, not now, not ever.

But as she looked at the warmth in his eyes she couldn't help but wonder why he'd betrayed her so comprehensively. Money, she'd assumed then—and goodness knows he'd needed it—but it still felt wrong, just as it had back then.

She'd headed straight to him at the time, desperate for answers, for a way out of the dark labyrinth she'd found herself trapped in. But there had been no comfort, just cold anger. He'd been the last person to turn on her—and he would stay the last person. She'd vowed it then, and she needed to remember it now.

But she couldn't punish the girls for their uncle's transgressions.

Alex forced a smile as she nodded at the eagerly listening child. 'It is. And then she'll live in a castle too. Just like you.'

Not that living in a castle was any indicator of happiness. She knew that better than anyone. But maybe the curse had disappeared with the Beaumonts. She hoped so for the girls' sake, if not Finn's.

'But I'm not a princess,' Saffron said sadly. 'Princesses are beautiful and clever.'

'Some are. But a real princess, a true princess, has a big heart and she fights for what's right.'

'She does?'

'Absolutely.'

Alex managed to stop herself rushing in to tell Saffron that she was beautiful. It wouldn't be a lie—the little girl was very pretty, with her tangle of dark hair and darker eyes—but, having been brought up knowing that her appeal lay in her looks and her precociousness, Alex had no intention of laying that burden on another Blakeley child.

Smiling reassuringly at Saffron, Alex looked up at the castle looming overhead and stifled the panic rearing inside her. This wasn't a good idea. She wasn't prepared. How could she be prepared?

But it didn't matter whether she was prepared or not because she was here. Here with the man who had administered the final kick ten years ago, making sure she was both down and out.

She had to remember that no matter how disarming his smile, how familiar the warmth in his dark, dark eyes, how protective he was of his nieces, it was all deceptive. All she could do was protect herself the way she always did. Concentrate on the job at hand and block out all other emotions.

And right now her job was getting some food and getting out of the castle as quickly as she could.

But, try as she might to stay cool and collected, she felt her heart start to beat a frantic and painful rhythm as they neared the side door leading into the boot room. From there, the well-trodden path led to the old scullery and then into the kitchen. The heart of the castle. Not a place either of her parents had ever ventured, unless her father had reverted to his school days and crept in to steal a still-warm cake from the huge walk-in pantry.

Ruled over by Mrs Atkinson, the kitchen had been a refuge, a stage and a home. Once ensconced at the kitchen table, Alex had known that she would be ordered to do her homework and sent off to bed at a reasonable time. It had been oddly satisfying.

'Is Mrs Atkinson still here?' she asked as she and Saffron joined Finn and Scarlett at the side door, after checking that the girls weren't listening. She didn't want them suspecting that she and Finn had a prior friendship, or that she wasn't the stranger to Blakeley she pretended to be.

'No, none of the castle staff stayed on afterwards.'

The word hung there. *Afterwards.* Just three syllables to sum up the dissolution of her entire life.

'I tried to persuade her to come back to run

the café, but she wasn't tempted. Too many ghosts, apparently.'

'That's a shame.'

Alex was split between relief that someone who would most definitely recognise her wasn't there to blow her cover and a surprisingly deep disappointment that she wouldn't be seeing one of the few people who had seemed to care about her when she was being just a normal child, not a precocious ingénue or a reckless daredevil.

She forced a smile. 'Her shortbread was legendary, and she'd never tell anyone the recipe. Your café would be a guaranteed success with her in the kitchen.'

She didn't usually chat so much, but talking helped mask the nerves tumbling through her body as Finn typed in a code on the back door and pushed it open, ushering her inside after the racing girls.

Alex blinked, recognition tingling in every nerve. Nothing had really changed. The same pegs on the walls, the same deep butler's sinks. The walls were a fresh white, the flagstones on the floor clean and oiled, and there were no dog bowls lining up against the far wall, but otherwise she could have been stepping back in time.

She swallowed as she followed Finn

through the scullery, now a smart-looking utility room, and into the kitchen.

'The oligarch really didn't remodel,' she managed to say through the ever-increasing lump in her throat.

Again, the kitchen was almost untouched. Buffed and painted and fresh, but with the same wooden cabinets and vast stove chucking out welcome heat. The same huge table dominated the centre. The table she had eaten at, drawn at, cried at more times than she could remember.

'No, he never came here. Everything was left as it was.'

'Until you came along to make it a new and improved model.'

She didn't want or mean to sound bitter. It was better that the castle was looked after. Of course it was. But why did it have to be Finn doing the looking after? And why did she have to be here, witnessing his success? Here on his payroll, her professional reputation in his hands, dependent on him for her evening meal.

None of it matters, she told herself, as she had so many times in the past. *None of it affects you.*

But the mantra didn't work. Not while she stood with the past all around her. The past in front of her. Finn had shed his winter coat and stood there in jeans and a close-fitting cashmere long-sleeved T-shirt. He'd filled out in the last few years. The snake-hipped passionate boy was now a lean but muscled man, eyes as dark and intent as ever, hair still falling over his brow.

For one treacherous moment something stirred inside her. Maybe her heart, maybe long-dormant desire. But she stood firm and pushed the feeling away. After all, hadn't this man hurt her the most? She couldn't, mustn't forget that. Ever. She'd worked too hard to move on.

She'd do her job to the best of her ability and leave, reputation and secret intact. No more cosy walks with Finn through the woods, no more trips down memory lane, and no recognising kindred spirits in small girls. It wasn't safe. The only time she would set foot in the castle after this evening would be to work.

Stick to the rules and she'd survive this. She had before and she'd do it again. She just needed to remember exactly who Finn Hawkin was.

CHAPTER FIVE

FINN LOOKED AROUND the crowded room, satisfaction running through him. All these people were here because of him. Journalists, influencers, local dignitaries, a scattering of celebrities. All drawn to Blakeley Castle once again.

Oh, he knew that many of them had only a passing interest in Hawk, in adventure trails, reinvigorating rural economies and bringing inner city kids into the countryside. They just wanted to set foot in the Blakeley Castle's legendary ballroom. To imagine they were one of the fabled generations of Bright Young Things who had danced, flirted, betrayed and seduced on this very floor.

Sometimes, at night, Finn would come in here and just for a moment catch a glimpse of a wisp of silk, a hint of taffeta, a flash of brocade. Every generation had its scandalous youth—whether they were Cavaliers, Regency beaux or jazz kids—and whatever the generation, whatever the scandal, they could all be found here at Blakeley.

But no more. His reign might be duller and more benign, but it would usher in a new tradition. One that was more inclusive. One with less misery in its wake.

Talking of which…

'Finn, here you are.'

Alex was playing the role of professional pen-pusher hard tonight. Finn knew that she hadn't lost her eye for fashion, or her taste, but there was no evidence of that eye or that taste tonight in the simple knee-length grey dress and matching jacket she wore. Her hair was tightly pulled back into a severe bun, a pair of black-rimmed glasses perched on her nose. She looked like a stock photo of a librarian rather than an attendee at a sought-after social event.

But Finn knew that her sartorial dullness was absolutely deliberate. After all, if her real identity was to be discovered then this was the time and place: back in her ancestral home surrounded by journalists. Not for the first time Finn wondered if he had done the right thing in bringing her back. Only this time it wasn't his peace of mind he was worried about. It was her anonymity. After all, hadn't he recognised her straight away?

But, then again, hadn't he known her better than anyone?

Alex ushered forward a petite woman. 'Can I introduce Isma Syed? Isma is the travel editor for the *Daily Courant* and she has a great blog as well—really inspiring and always ahead of the crowd. She's one of Blakeley's first guests too. She's spending the night in the Dower House.'

'Pleased to meet you.' Finn smiled at Isma, whose dark eyes were bright with interest. 'I hope you've enjoyed the day so far—and that the accommodation is up to your expectations?'

'It's very comfortable, thank you. And, yes! I wasn't sure that a treetop trail was really my thing, but I enjoyed it far more than I expected. So, Finn, how does it feel to come home? You grew up here, didn't you?'

It was no secret. 'My family have lived here for generations,' Finn agreed.

'But not in the castle itself? Do you know how the Beaumonts feel about the gardener becoming the Lord of the Manor?'

Finn sensed rather than saw Alex stiffen beside him. 'I haven't had an opportunity to discuss it with them, but I hope they would be pleased to know that the castle is being looked after by someone who loves it as much as they did…someone who has an ancestral affinity for the place.'

'Of course.' Isma leaned forward, her voice lowered confidentially. 'Lord Beaumont is dead and there were no male heirs. That's why the castle was for sale in the first place. But what about Lady Beaumont and her daughter? Do you have any idea where Lola Beaumont is right now?'

Lying didn't come easily to Finn, but he hadn't brought Alex here to embarrass her or, worse, to expose her to the media, no matter what he had said earlier that week when persuading her to stay.

'As far as I know Lady Beaumont is still in California. As for Lola, I haven't heard from her for many years. So, how does the Dower House compare with other holiday cottages you've seen? Any suggestions on how we can improve things?'

'Ah, you'll have to wait for my review. I hear you're also reviving the famous Christmas Eve party?'

Finn nodded. 'It is a Blakeley tradition.'

'But do you think it's wise? After all, the last party ended with the drowning of Lord

Beaumont's mistress and that started it all…'
She raised her eyebrows in query.

Finn was very careful not to look at Alex
as he answered, focusing all his charm on
the journalist. 'This is a new era at Blakeley
and the party will reflect that. We are planning more of a community affair, including
carols sung by the local primary school choir
and a village nativity. Have you had a chance
to look around the castle yet? Nearly all of
it is publicly accessible now, from the ser-
vants' quarters to the room where Elizabeth
I is reputed to have had a secret liaison, and
it's all exactly as it has been for the last four
hundred-odd years.'

Isma stepped forward, her phone in her
hand, no doubt ready to record, her expression avid. 'Of course Blakeley is famous for
its liaisons. When you lived here before did
people know about what went on at the parties the Beaumonts held? The wife-swapping,
the orgies, the drugs? The mountain of debt
their lifestyle was built on? I mean, you were
right here. You must have seen things? Heard
things? What about Lola? You were around
the same age. Did she ever pull a Lady Chat-
terley with the staff?'

Finn tensed. *Great.* The travel reporter was
hot on the scent and Finn couldn't blame her.

The drowning of a pop star's model wife at one of the most famous events in the social calendar had been the scandal of the year ten years ago.

The Blakely Christmas Eve party had always been filled with an eclectic mix of aristocracy, minor royalty, actors and musicians, a mecca for the rich, beautiful and cool. When it had been revealed that the dead woman was Lord Beaumont's lover—and that his own wife had been having an affair with the much younger pop star—the scandal had blown sky-high. Stories of years of excess had circulated, and at some point Lord Beaumont's debts had surfaced. Facing ruin, he had shot himself, and his wife had fled to LA with her lover, leaving her daughter alone to deal with the debts, with the press, with the scandal.

At that point Lola might have turned things round. She had been young, beautiful, and making a name for herself as a model, an It Girl. If she'd wanted to she could have ridden out the storm and kept her influential friends, her endorsements and her contracts. But then the photos had surfaced. Photos of her at that very same Christmas Eve party on her eighteenth birthday. Photos not meant for the public to see.

Photos for Finn's eyes only.

It was strange how she had been able to pose in a barely-there bikini, her almost nude body up on a billboard, and nobody had blinked. That was *fashion*. But private photos, in which she exposed more or less the same amount of skin, were salacious just because of their private nature.

And they'd been everywhere. Front pages, comedy panel shows, opinion pieces. The sins of her parents had been put squarely on her shoulders. She had become a symbol of everything that was wrong in a world that at the time had been facing a recession. The Beaumonts' excessive consumption had been held up as an example of a world that needed fixing.

Still she might have stayed and fought. If it hadn't been for the fact that only one person had had access to those photos.

Finn.

He glanced across at Alex, standing by the journalist's side, her face absolutely impervious, as if none of the things the journalist had said affected her at all. As if she really was someone completely different not just in name but in every way. Someone so closed down there was no knowing what, if anything, she was thinking. It was as if she was sleepwalking through life.

'I'm sorry, I didn't really take much notice of anything that happened in the castle. Too busy focusing on my future.'

His smile was tight as Alex turned to the journalist, as ever the consummate professional. Did none of this affect her at all? But then she hadn't asked to be put into this position. He had put her there. How could he judge her for the way she handled it?

'Isma, can I introduce you to Desiree?' Alex was saying. 'She's got over two hundred and fifty thousand Instagram followers and is thinking about writing a book about her love of travel. I said that you were absolutely the person to speak to. Your book about your year travelling solo was my favourite read last year…it was so inspirational. Thank you, Finn.'

And with a polite but firm smile Alex steered Isma away.

Finn took a glass of Prosecco from the table next to him and drank it down in one long gulp, closing his eyes briefly. He hadn't had a chance to talk to Alex about the photos, to make the explanation he should have forced her to listen to back then. At the time he'd been so angry and hurt that she'd believed him capable of such betrayal he hadn't been able to see how devastated she was, unable to see the wood for the trees as her world collapsed around her. Everyone and everything she had known was a lie. No wonder she'd thought him a lie as well.

It was too late to repair the damage. But it wasn't too late to tell her the truth.

Finn watched Alex as she introduced Isma to a striking young woman dressed in an eye-catching jumpsuit. The two women immediately fell into animated conversation and Alex stepped back, her clear gaze sweeping the room, making sure everyone was having a good time, talking to the right people, looking for anything that might need to be explained or contained.

Her disguise was completely effective. No one spared her a second glance.

It wasn't the glasses. They couldn't hide her long lashes or her large grey eyes with their provocative tilt, as if she was smiling at a joke only she could see. The severe bun couldn't disguise the glossiness of her hair, and her tall, lean curves weren't diminished by the unflattering cut and colour of her suit.

No, her beauty was as stunning as it had ever been, and no amount of stereotyped frumpy clothes could change that. It was inside. She was switched off. There was no vibrancy lighting her, no animation, and that was why she could slip through the crowds unseen.

But Finn saw her. He always had.

Alex inhaled as she looked around. Everything was in order. The ballroom was festively decorated, with fairy lights strung around the panelling, and a large Christmas tree dominated the far corner, tastefully blazing with white and silver lights, wrapped presents clustered at the bottom. So the presents were empty boxes? It didn't matter. This evening, like all this kind of occasion, was an illusion. The journalists, influencers and assembled celebrities were there to be charmed and to spread the word: Blakeley Castle was open once again.

Of course conversation turned again and again to the last owners. Who were Elizabeth I or Charles II or Beau Brummel compared to the disgraced Viscount and his family? But no one gossiping about the events of ten years ago really thought about the cost—about the two people who had died, about the families torn apart. The Blakeley scandal was like something out of a novel, not real life.

Only she knew all too well just how real it had been. No one else could ever know or understand what it had been like in the centre of that hurricane, with her life whirling more and more out of control, everyone wanting a piece of her.

Alex shivered, aware that she was being watched, Looking up, she saw Finn's dark gaze fixed unwaveringly on her. As if he saw *her*, not the woman she had worked so hard to be but the girl she had left behind her. That needy creature who had thought beauty and praise worth having, who hadn't understood how fleeting and insubstantial they were.

How dared he look at her that way? He had lost the right to see her the day he had betrayed her. What game was he playing anyway? How had he tracked her down? And how could she trust him not to betray her again?

The room was too hot, too busy. She needed to regroup. Slipping out of a side door, she let her feet lead her unerringly through the maze of corridors, up the stairs, until she reached the long picture gallery, still hung with portraits of her ancestors.

Alex stood in the cool, dim light and looked around. Thank goodness that oligarch had bought the castle complete with all its contents—she would have hated for the pictures to have been sold off and separated, to hang in museums and private collections, even though the money raised would have been enough to pay off her father's debts and give her a nest egg to rebuild her life.

The gallery had been included in the tour of the house laid on for the party guests, and she had stood here in this room several times already today, but she hadn't allowed herself to look up, to be distracted, to remember how she'd used to come here and chat to her favourite pictures. Now, alone, she walked slowly from picture to picture. There was the Gainsborough, the Reynolds, the Holbein... Every ancestor had the same smile, the same sleepy cat eyes she herself had inherited, the same pointed chin.

'Hi,' she whispered softly to the spaniel hiding in one lady's skirts. 'Sorry I haven't been to visit for a while. Hello, handsome.' She reached a hand up to a grey horse, not quite touching it. As a child these painted animals had been her confidants and playmates. These animals—and Finn.

She wandered slowly up the long panelled gallery, reuniting with old friends, stopping to say hello to her favourites until she reached the end, where she stilled, barely breathing, her heart squeezing in on itself until her whole chest ached.

The huge painting of a nude with long red hair and a slanting smile dominated the room. Some had called her the most beautiful woman in the world. She could have married royalty or wealth, a Hollywood star or a business king, but she had chosen a boy with a minor title and a castle, and she had reigned over that castle with whimsical tyranny.

Alex stared up at the painting, at the creamy skin, the curve of perfect pert breasts, the come-hither glance in green, green eyes. 'Hi, Mum,' she said.

The portrait stared impassively back. No different from its sitter. Alex could count on one hand the conversations she had had with her mother since that last tragic Christmas Eve.

After breaking up with her pop star lover, the former Lady Beaumont had married an actor some years her senior. They now lived on a ranch with their two children, where her mother ran an online health and wellbeing empire. A disgraced daughter who was a living reminder of a past much better left behind didn't fit with the brand she'd so painstakingly built up.

Occasionally, very occasionally, Alex would scroll through her social media feed, full of nutritious homemade food and yoga poses, outdoor living and glowing, laughing children, and search for clues. Were her unknown half-siblings really happy, or did they too spend their lives waiting for a nod or a smile, desperately trying to please their capricious beautiful mother? Trying to be the perfect child and always, always falling short?

She didn't really want an answer. She would hate for them to be raised the way she had been, but on the other hand, if her mother genuinely loved her new family, did that mean there was something wrong with Alex? That she was fundamentally unlovable?

History tended to bear that assumption out.

Swallowing, she turned her back on her mother, smothering a gasp as she saw two white figures at the far end of the gallery. 'Saffron! Scarlett, you startled me,' she said, half laughing with nerves. 'Aren't you supposed to be in bed? You must be freezing,' she added as she took in their bare feet and thin white pyjamas.

'Not as cold as that lady.' Scarlett giggled as she pointed at the portrait of Alex's mother.

'True. At least you're wearing *some* clothes.' Alex managed to keep a straight face.

'Who is she? Is she a princess? And why isn't she wearing any clothes?'

'Not a princess, but she used to be married to someone who lived here. It's considered artistic to paint people without clothes, for some reason, and she was a very famous beauty.'

'I think she looks mean,' Saffron said suddenly. 'Like a wicked witch or a bad godmother who casts an evil spell.'

Alex swivelled to look back at the portrait, at the sensuous look in the famously hooded eyes, the knowing expression. 'Yes,' she said slowly. 'I suppose she does.'

'Alex, Alex, come and look at your picture!'

Before Alex could make her excuses and head back to the ballroom, Scarlett had run up to slip one small, cold hand in hers and begun to tug her towards the small antechamber where the castle's prized collection of Pre-Raphaelite paintings hung.

'Quickly,' she agreed. 'But then straight back to bed. It's far too cold—and late—for you two to be running around the castle.'

Hypocrite, she told herself. As if *she* hadn't spent many nights roaming the castle when other children her age had been fast asleep. But she would have loved someone to scoop her up and order her back to bed. Freedom palled when it was mixed with indifference.

'Will you read us a story?' Scarlett asked.

Alex looked down at the small heart-shaped face and the pleading expression in her dark eyes. She didn't know any children, and rarely needed to interact with them. Amber loved nothing more than organising a child's party or entertaining their younger clients, but Alex never knew what to say to them…how to be.

'I really need to get back and do my job,' she said.

'Don't be silly, Scarlett. Alex is far too busy to bother with us.'

There was a resigned loneliness in Saffron's sneer, one Alex recognised all too well.

'Let me check for messages,' she said. 'If no one has tried to contact me then one story. Okay?'

For once her phone showed no urgent messages or red-flagged emails.

'One short story,' she warned them. 'Before I'm missed.'

'Picture first,' Scarlett said.

Alex allowed herself to be towed into the dimly lit room where the Beaumont collection of Pre-Raphaelite paintings was displayed. She couldn't help but gasp in recognition as she looked at the jewel-like colours on the six perfectly displayed paintings. They weren't the best known, or the most critically well regarded, but it didn't matter because they were all set here at Blakeley.

The nymph in the lake eying up a young Narcissus was standing in Blakeley water. The goddess hiding from Actaeon's gaze stood in the woods Alex had walked through today on her way to the office. And the sleeping maiden, her hair falling to the floor, her nightgown dipping below one perfect white breast, a rose in her hand, slumbered in Alex's old bedchamber, on the Victorian bedstead where she had once slept.

'See, she looks like you,' Scarlett said triumphantly.

Saffron nodded. 'She does. If you weren't wearing glasses and if you grew your hair really long.'

'And I wore a see-through nightie and forgot to do it up properly? Sorry, girls. I'm a more of a scrunched-up ponytail and yoga pants kind of nightwear person.'

To her surprise both girls laughed at her weak attempt at humour, and the bell-like sound echoed off the panelled walls, warming the frigid air.

'Come on,' she said, taking Scarlett's hand and touching Saffron's shoulder. 'If you want me to read a story before I have to go back to the party—and before you both turn into blocks of ice—then we need to get you back to bed.'

But before she went she allowed herself one last lingering glance at the slumbering girl. At the stained glass in the window behind her and the way the light played across her supine figure. At the little dog curled up at his mistress's side. At the anticipation on the sleeper's face, the way her lips were parted ready. At the shadow at the window, the glimpse of thorns and the determined man ready to slash through them.

Some people thought the story insipid—a heroine who merely fell asleep and waited to be rescued—but Alex had always thought it the ultimate romance that no matter how lost you were, someone would find you. That you could be hidden behind one hundred years' worth of trees and thorns and someone would still see you, know you and fight for you.

She no longer felt like that. Now she knew better. Now she knew the only person to fight for you was you. And that sometimes the only way to do that, the only way to save yourself, was to retreat and keep all the things that could hurt you at bay. No hope, no love, no dreams.

But for one moment, as she walked through corridors she knew better than she knew her heart, listening to the chatter of two over-excited girls, she allowed herself to wish, just briefly, that she still believed in fairy-tales.

CHAPTER SIX

'ALEX!'

Alex turned at the sound of the high-pitched voice and saw a small child speeding towards her. It had turned even colder over the last few days and the trees glistened with morning frost, the grass crunchy white underfoot.

'Good morning, Scarlett.' She caught the small girl before she barrelled into her, suppressing a smile at the layers of clothing, the thick padded jacket, hat and gloves and the bright orange wellies on her small feet. 'Living the Hawk brand, I see.'

'Of course.'

Finn caught up with them and her breath caught in her throat. It was most unfair that he had turned out even more attractive than the boy she had loved, especially with his chin coated with overnight stubble, his hair tousled and his expression relaxed.

'Thanks for the other night,' he added. 'The press party seemed to go very well.'

'I'm never satisfied until I see all the reviews but I'm cautiously optimistic,' Alex agreed. 'Thank goodness the weather held for the afternoon. I'm not sure treetop treks and biking woodland trails would have been so much fun in the rain. It's just a shame the nature walk looks so bare at this time of year, but the interpretation was really good, so they got the gist of what you want to achieve.'

'The tweaks you made really enhanced the whole experience, especially housing some of the journalists here—even the ones in the Bunkhouse seemed to have fun, judging from the comments I heard at breakfast yesterday. Thank you.'

'Just doing my job.'

'It wasn't your job to return these two scamps to their bed, though.' Finn glared mock sternly at his nieces, and they shrieked and rushed along the path ahead. 'Thank you for keeping them out of trouble. That was above and beyond.'

'It was no problem. They're nice girls.' She paused, not wanting to prolong the conversation or bring up any more shared memories, but her curiosity overran her good sense.

'They must miss their mum. Where is Nicky? She was pregnant when I...'

Dammit, this was where curiosity took her. Right back to that night. And there were so many reasons not to go back to that night. Self-preservation for one.

Self-preservation took many routes. It meant not thinking about watching her father stagger out of the lake with a lifeless body in his arms. It meant not remembering the media storm, the reporters at every gate. It meant not reliving her rigid fear, sitting in the back of a police car as she was taken in for questioning, camera flashes blinding her.

And self-preservation meant not thinking about the photos or the moment she saw them all over the front pages. It meant remembering that this man couldn't be trusted, no matter how warm his gaze as it fell on his nieces, how attractive his crinkled smile.

A smile that was currently playing around his mouth as he watched Scarlett gravely hopscotching along the path leading through the woodland.

'Nicky finally signed over custody to me this summer.' As he spoke the smile disappeared and Finn's jaw set firm, his mouth a grim line, his eyes unreadable.

'Custody? You mean she isn't around at all?'

'She's flitted in and out of their lives for years. Every time she swears she's made a change. So I set her up in a house, make sure there's enough money for the girls, and then she meets another loser. Next thing I know he's moved in or she's moved out, and six months later the girls are returned to me for another "holiday" while she sorts herself out. It might be two weeks, it might be a month, or longer. I've had enough of enabling her. They need stability. Especially Saffy.'

'Yes. I see. She does seem fragile.'

They walked a little further in silence before Finn spoke again, his words tense and clipped. 'I should have done something sooner, said something sooner, but I didn't want to alienate Nicky. They were her daughters…what if she banned me from seeing them? And, despite everything, I wanted to believe that her heart was in the right place. She protected me, you know, from the worst of my dad's drinking. Even when she did something wrong her motives were good. I had to keep giving her the benefit of the doubt. But then Saffy…' He stopped and rubbed his hand against his jaw.

'Then Saffy what?'

Finn sighed, and she could see the indecision in his eyes as he weighed up whether or not to answer.

'She reminded me of you,' he said at last.

Alex's breath caught at his words, chills numbing her every nerve.

'That look you had when your parents would go away and you'd be waiting for them to come back, or when your mum barely knew you were there. That hopeful look. It used to break my heart then, but seeing it replicated on Saffy...' He shook his head, lost in some memory. 'I was no longer a boy. I have money, and a home, and I can give her the stability she needs. I thought Nicky would fight me for them, and I was prepared to involve the courts if I had to. Even though I know she loves them. But she just gave in.'

'Maybe she gave in *because* she loves them. Because she knows it's for the best.'

But Alex's heart was hammering so loudly she could hardly hear herself speak. She'd always thought she'd hidden her fear of rejection from everyone, including Finn. She'd worked so hard to be the smiling, impetuous, devil-may-care child her parents had wanted. Never cried, never sulked, never followed the rules. Charming, wild and beautiful. A Beaumont through and through.

Beaumonts didn't need or ask for approval

and they felt stifled by rules and stability. Alex had done her very best to feel stifled too. But if Finn had seen it was all a pretence had others seen it too? Her parents?

'Maybe,' said Finn. 'I'd already bought Blakeley and I started to invest in turning it into the kind of outdoor centre I wanted it to be, decided to stop travelling so much. Moving my life here properly made perfect sense. The girls can go to the local schools. Stop chopping and changing, stay in one place.'

'And Nicky doesn't see them at all?'

'She's in India right now, but she can see them whenever she wants for as long as she wants when she's in the UK. So long as it's here. She has a bedroom here that's hers alone—not that she's even seen it. But the girls stay with me until they are out of formal education. That's the agreement.'

'Wow. That's a big commitment.'

'I didn't have a choice. I couldn't let them down. I've done enough of that. Letting people I care about down.'

His words hung in the air until Alex could hardly breathe. Did he mean his father, belligerent and difficult, refusing all offers of help? Or his sister, searching for an elusive happiness even her children couldn't provide? Or was he talking about back then? When he'd promised to be her knight but ended up her betrayer?

'No, you had a choice and you chose them. Even with money and a home that's an unselfish choice to make. Being a single parent is hard even when children have always known love and stability.'

'Which is why they come first. Their happiness is paramount.'

'Of course.'

Despite everything that hung between them, all that lay unsaid, all the secrets and lies and betrayals, she couldn't help but admire Finn for his dedication—and she allowed herself one tiny wish: that someone had put her first when she'd still needed somebody to care.

Once again Finn found Alex almost impossible to read. She had been curious about the girls, understandably, and she had sounded sympathetic whilst asking questions, but there was still an otherworldly air around her, as if she were miles away from here, in a different existence entirely.

That was probably what made her so good at her job. That sense she was somehow remote, untouched, that nothing really affected her. He'd seen her at work during the press party. Always watching, introducing, stepping in with a cool smile and a light but steely touch, making sure every message stayed on brand, that the assembled journalists experienced what she wanted them to experience. So unlike the girl he'd known, who had felt everything so very deeply a harsh word could cut her.

But only he had known that. She had been so adept at hiding her true nature. Did she still hide now? It was impossible to tell. But for a moment he badly wanted to find out.

'Uncle Finn, can Alex help us choose our tree?'

Scarlett appeared at his side, her cheeks the same colour as her name, her hair once again a tangled mess.

He passed a rueful hand over the curls. 'I need an uncle school to teach me how to do plaits,' he said.

'I told you. Emily's dad watched online videos and he can wind ribbons through her hair. You just have to try harder,' Scarlett told him.

He tugged one messy plait. 'Message understood.'

'So can she?' She turned eagerly to Alex. 'We get to choose our very own tree from our very own woods and then we take it back and decorate it. And Uncle Finn has all these amazing Christmas tree ornaments; he collects them everywhere he goes.'

Alex stilled, her cheeks paling. 'I used to collect Christmas tree ornaments,' she said softly.

'Do you still have them?'

'No. Not any more. I had to leave them behind when I left home. And some I gave away.'

Finn curled his hand into a loose fist as she steadfastly avoided looking at him, but he knew they were thinking of the same time. Of her first modelling job in New York, when she was barely fifteen and barely chaperoned by her mother. She'd brought him back an ornament from a world-famous department store: a perfect glass apple. Far too delicate for his Christmas tree, and far too beautiful for a seventeen-year-old boy whose focus had been on school and getting out. But he had thanked her, and from then on, on every trip to every place, she had brought home two Christmas tree ornaments: one for him and one for her to keep.

He still had every one.

'So, can she?' Scarlett asked.

Finn searched for an excuse, a reason to let Alex off the hook, but before he could speak Saffy mooched up to them, her thin shoulders hunched under her anorak.

'Are we going to choose this tree or not?'

'I was just explaining to Alex what we are doing,' Scarlett said with extraordinary dignity. 'And inviting her along to be one of the party.'

Finn looked at Alex, startled into a shout of laughter, and saw answering laughter soften her grey eyes, her mouth grow full and sweet with the natural curve of her smile. His breath caught in his throat. She had been a beautiful girl, but she had grown into a glorious woman. When she allowed herself to be natural. When her smile had meaning.

His pulse began to thud as he stared, unable to look away, drinking in the sight. He didn't care what she called herself, this was the only woman who had ever made his blood thrill; the only woman to make his heart thump so loud he was convinced it could be heard back at the castle; the only woman his hands ached to touch so badly the pain was physical. He knew how she tasted. Sweet and fresh and lush, like nectar. How she felt. Warm silk and soft velvet. And she knew him as well. For all she denied it.

'Uncle Finn!' Scarlett's insistent voice brought him out of his reverie and he stared at her and blinked. 'Ask Alex to join us.'

And Finn realised that he wanted nothing

more. Not just because of that shared conspiratorial moment of amusement, or because of the sudden visceral memories that had blindsided him, but because he suspected that Alexandra Davenport was even lonelier than Lola Beaumont had been.

'Of course,' he said easily, taking Saffron's hand. 'If you have nothing better to do.'

'I…'

'You might as well,' Saffy said, staring down at the ground, and Finn saw Alex's expression soften with recognition.

'Only if you're sure I'm not intruding.'

'Yay!' Scarlett started dancing around, hair flying. 'Come on, Alex. After we choose the tree we're going to decorate it and have hot chocolate with cream and it's going to be the best day ever.'

She flew off down the path, tugging a startled-looking Alex with her, and Finn followed on more sedately, still holding Saffron's mittened hand.

'Do you mind, Saffy?' he said gently. 'I know today is meant to be a family day…'

A life filled with 'uncles' and 'new daddies' had left Saffron wary of outsiders, especially ones who tried to step into her inner circle. But to his surprise Saffy shook her head.

'Alex is nice. She's really good at reading stories too. She did all the voices. Even though it was a babyish story of Scarlett's she made it seem really funny.'

'That's good. As long as you're okay, Saffy.'

His niece rolled her eyes in the pre-teen way she had perfected recently. 'I'm fine. Come on, Uncle Finn, bet I can beat you.'

And she was off, too-long skinny legs pumping furiously as she sped down the path, ponytail flying out behind her.

With a mock roar of rage Finn took off after her, but underneath a beat of anxiety pounded insistently. The girls had been hurt enough. It was good that they liked Alex, but she would be leaving at Christmas. He had to make sure they didn't get too attached.

And it wasn't just them he needed to watch. Having Alex back at Blakeley felt too right, too easy, especially when he saw glimpses of the girl he'd used to know. But they were both different people now, with very different lives, and far too old to believe in happy-ever-afters.

It was surprisingly easy to find and agree on the right tree, and before an hour had passed they were all back in the castle for the promised hot chocolate, the tree cut and delivered by one of the estate hands.

Alex paused as they left the kitchen, uncertainty on her face as the girls rushed into the sitting room. 'Are you sure it's okay for me to be here?'

'More than sure. I need someone to help carry these mugs.' Finn nodded at the large mugs filled with hot chocolate he'd just made, topped with cream and sprinkles, and slipped a packet of shortbread into his pocket before picking up two of them.

'Biscuits not served on plates? Mrs Atkinson would be horrified,' Alex said. 'Shop bought as well.'

'If you want to make some from scratch you're very welcome to try.'

Finn grinned as she shook her head.

'Amber's the baker in our house. She bakes to relax, which means there is always fresh bread and cakes and biscuits all over the kitchen. I'm dreading Emilia and Harriet moving out, leaving me to face temptation all alone.'

'Send her to me. Feeding two growing girls is exhausting. I feel like a mother bird, constantly pushing worms into open mouths.'

'What a lovely analogy.'

She picked up the remaining two mugs and slipped through the door he held open with his foot and into the sitting room, pausing uncertainly as she reached the threshold of what he knew was a room once familiar to her.

In her day this had been the family room, a space used only by Alex, Finn and Mrs Atkinson. Her parents had rarely set foot in the domestic quarters. They had used the entire castle with careless entitlement, sitting on sixteenth-century chairs and sleeping in beds older than entire family trees. They had thought nothing of dancing on priceless carpets or leaving glasses on Chippendale tables.

But the rooms and their contents had all been painstakingly cleaned and restored, and now the whole castle was open to the public. All except the west wing, which he'd turned into a spacious, comfortable home.

'This looks amazing.' Alex halted as she stepped into the sitting room. 'I can't believe the difference. Look how beautiful the floor is!'

Finn had opened the room up into the old dining room beyond to create a large, welcoming space, with grouped sofas and chairs, a huge fireplace, and filled bookshelves in every alcove. Cushion-covered window seats ran the length of the room, and the pale grey of the walls showcased the bright, modern paintings he'd chosen.

All the furniture in their living space had been bought especially, and every room was newly painted, every floor stripped and polished. He'd wanted a blank canvas, a new start, with no hint of the old aristocratic family imposing on his.

The only part of the west wing that hadn't been renovated was the long picture gallery which ran the entire second floor of the wing. That he *hadn't* opened up to public view, despite the fame of some of the portraits.

He hadn't allowed himself to wonder why. But seeing Alex here, back in her home, he knew why. He hadn't wanted to rake up the old scandal again with every visitor. He hadn't wanted them to look at the cat-shaped eyes and pointed chins of her ancestors and remember her, gossip about her. Without knowing it he'd protected her, as he had failed to do so long ago.

He set the mugs on a small table and looked over at the huge tree set in a corner of the room. 'Okay,' he said, trying to push the past back where it belonged. 'Who wants to decorate the tree?'

'Me! Me!'

The girls nearly upset their hot chocolate in their bid to get to the box of ornaments first.

'Thank goodness John put the lights on

when he brought the tree in,' said Alex, her eyes narrowed in amusement as she watched the girls delve into the large box Finn had brought down from the box room earlier. 'They might have combusted if they'd had to wait any longer.'

She wrapped her hands around the large mug, lowering her nose to the fragrant chocolate and inhaling deeply.

'Thank you, Finn.'

'For what? The hot chocolate? I was making it anyway.'

But she didn't respond to his teasing smile. 'For not telling anyone who I am.'

'Alex…' Her name felt natural now. It suited this new incarnation. It was a name as anonymous as she seemed to be, yet with so many different layers and interpretations. 'It is completely within my interests to keep your secret. I want people to talk about Blakeley—of course I do. But I want them to talk about the local produce in the farm shop and the scones in the café, the treetop trail and the treasure hunt in the house, not to be sidetracked by old gossip. I'd much prefer that no one has the faintest idea who you are.'

'Then why hire me? And how did you even track me down?'

Finn inhaled, the scent of chocolate mixing

with the pine tree and permeating the room. So, they were going to have this conversation. Well, maybe it was time. Maybe it was time he finally told her the truth. Maybe it was time to set the past free.

'Finn? I think I deserve some answers.'

'Yes,' he agreed. 'You do.'

CHAPTER SEVEN

'How did you find me?' Alex repeated. She fixed her gaze on him firmly and waited.

Finn slanted a look towards Saffron and Scarlett, but they were intent on the tree, deliberating over where a Christmas angel Alex recognised as one she'd picked up in Prague should go. She'd never expected that he would still have the ornaments she'd bought him. Never expected to see them hung on a tree in Blakeley Castle. It shook all that she'd thought she knew. About him, about them.

She swallowed and waited some more. He set his hot chocolate down on a side table and leaned against the sofa arm, looking out of the window at the white mist swirling along the frost-covered lawn.

'Returning to Blakeley brought back old memories,' he said abruptly. 'But I had my own personal reasons to return. Reasons that have nothing to do with you. My ancestors are as much a part of this castle as yours, even if no one really cares about the people who spent their lives in the kitchens and the gardens, no matter how many generations they dedicated to serving the castle.'

'I care. And I don't dispute your claim on Blakeley. If I can't be here to look after the castle, then there's no one I'd rather it should be than you.'

'Really?'

His eyebrows rose in disbelief, but she nodded, reinforcing her statement.

'Finn, how can anyone *own* history? We're only ever custodians of a place like Blakeley. Now the castle has a custodian who loves her and knows her, respects her. That's a wonderful thing.'

She meant every word, but her chest ached with loss and regret as she spoke. She hoped he didn't sense her wistfulness, saw only her sincerity.

'Thank you. That means a lot.'

'So?' she prompted. 'You're back here and you need a temporary PR person and what? It's a huge coincidence that you chose me.'

'No. Not a coincidence. I've known where you are for six months.'

She froze. 'That long? How? Why? Were you looking for me?'

Damn it, was that hope she was feeling? Hope that he had been searching for her? That she hadn't been lost after all?

'Not straight away.' He stopped abruptly, jaw tightening. 'I should have,' he said, his voice resonant with regret. 'I should have come straight after you at the time…shouldn't have allowed you to walk away without an explanation. But for the first few days afterwards I was too hurt, too angry to speak to you. You were so sure I was guilty. After all we had been to each other, after all we'd said, you thought I'd sell photos of you to the press. *Those* photos.'

The utter disbelief in his expression floored her. Hurt and anger were still evident in that disbelief. Had she got it so wrong? But who else could it have been? She'd sent the photos to him, not to anyone else…

'I'd have given anything for it not to be you. The papers were full of people who I'd trusted, who I'd thought cared about me, spilling every last sordid detail about my family. You needed money. You said so yourself. To help Nicky, to get to university…'

'And so I sold you for thirty pieces of silver? Did you really believe that? Do you still?'

'I…'

Of course she had. It had been the last revelation. The one that had tipped her from holding on to falling, falling into a dark, dark place. But now? Seeing all he had achieved, and more importantly what he was doing with that success—opening up the estate, working with inner city schools, raising his nieces… These were the actions of a decent man, not a man who would betray someone who'd loved him.

And, truthfully, nothing he had done back then had shown him to be capable of such an act. He'd been her one constant after all.

'Finn…' But she couldn't speak, and the silence thickened, broken only by the chatter of the girls, their words washing over Alex.

'I waited too long,' he said after a while. 'I waited for you to come back and apologise. And by the time I could see more clearly, by the time I understood, you had disappeared.'

'What did you understand?' she whispered; throat thick with fear. She wasn't sure she could cope with his answer.

'I understood that you needed to blame someone for the way things fell apart. How could you blame your dad when he was no longer around to blame? And you always made every excuse for your mother. You had to blame me. I had to be the scapegoat. I knew that it was up to me, that I had to go to you. But, even though it had been just a few days since I'd seen you last, I couldn't find you anywhere. Not in any of the usual places, not with any of the usual people. In the end I told myself that you would show up eventually. I hoped to see you back in the gossip columns and on billboards within months, riding out the scandal. But months went by and you didn't appear in any headlines or adverts. It was as if you had been airbrushed out of existence and I knew I had lost you in every way possible. It didn't stop me hoping that one day you would turn up, that I would see you again, but finally I had to accept that you didn't want me to find you, that you didn't want anyone. I had to do my best to move on, to build my business and my life.'

Alex stood stock-still, her mind digesting every word he'd said, turning each phrase over and over and trying to make sense of it all. 'You *had* to have sold them,' she said. 'I only sent them to you. You needed money and you had them. There was no one else.'

He folded his arms and said nothing, but she saw his eyes flicker towards the still absorbed girls and clarity almost blinded her.

'It was Nicky.'

'Yes.'

'Nicky…'

Of course. She would have been able to access Finn's phone—goodness knew he'd always been mislaying it. She'd needed money and she'd always disliked Alex. How had she not realised at the time? Maybe Finn was right. She had had to blame someone and he'd been right there, her one constant. She'd lashed out and driven him away just when she needed him most.

All this time she'd thought he had betrayed her, but *she* had betrayed him. The ache in her chest intensified, constricting her and making it hard to breathe. 'Finn, I—'

But he held up a hand to cut her off. 'Don't. Like I said, you needed a scapegoat. I was there. It's fine. It was long ago. I moved on and moved out, after realising my presence here wasn't going to save my father or change Nicky. I needed to start working for the future I'd always promised myself. To concentrate on university and a life of my own.'

'You've achieved that, all right.' Alex looked around at the original pieces of art on the walls, at the two happy girls, giggling over a bauble. 'Achieved so much. You should be so proud.'

'But I never stopped thinking about you. I've always known I could have done more, should have done more when you needed me. I hoped you were with your mother in the States, happy and fulfilled, but I always knew that was a long shot.' He sighed. 'I just wanted closure, I suppose. This last year, worrying about Saffy, buying the castle, just made me realise I hadn't really moved on, that maybe I never completely would.'

'Did you hire a detective?'

Alex sat on the window seat, her back to the wall, needing as much physical support as she could get. Because if Finn could track her down, then who else could? With the renewed interest in Blakeley it was surely a matter of time before another *Where is Lola?* piece ran. What if a journalist really wanted answers? Look at Isma, just a couple of days ago, not even suspecting that the woman she wanted was standing right there.

'No. I considered it, several times, especially at the beginning. But back then I couldn't afford it, and later it didn't seem right...not when you had gone to such lengths to disappear. I tried to resign myself to living with the guilt, with never knowing, but I couldn't stop myself looking for you wherever I went, ridiculous as I knew that was. And then I was invited to a ball...'

'A ball?' She couldn't hide her surprise. It so wasn't the answer she'd been expecting.

Alex quickly ran through a mental list of all the charity balls she had helped organise over the last few months.

'A Midsummer Ball. The invite came from a guy I studied with briefly at the Sorbonne—a guy who just happens to be an archduke.'

Alex nodded slowly. All the pieces were coming together. 'Laurent?'

'Laurent,' he confirmed. 'At one point I was talking to him and he was so busy staring at a woman—your friend—he was barely focussing on what I was saying. When I looked over too, she was talking to a tall woman dressed in black. A woman I knew instantly. Although she had a different name, I knew that Alexandra Davenport and Lola Beaumont were the same person.'

'Why didn't you come and see me? Pick up the phone? Why make me come here after everything?'

'Because in just the brief glimpse I had of you it seemed that you had changed fundamentally, Alex. Not just your name, but you. It was as if the fire that used to fuel you had gone out. It got me wondering if I wasn't the only one who needed closure. I spent the next six months wondering what the right move would be—and of course I had the girls to settle into their new schools, the move of the business to manage, the opening up of the castle. Part of me wondered if you would hear about what was happening at Blakeley and contact me. Then Penelope was injured, and it just seemed the time was right. When I phoned that evening I thought I'd speak to you, so when Amber picked up it threw me somewhat. That was why I said I'd brief you when you got here. I wondered if you would simply refuse to come, but it didn't cross my mind that you had no idea I'd hired you.'

As he finished, he picked up their cups and headed back to the kitchen. Alex watched the door swing shut. She shivered. Sitting there in her old family room, with the past excavated, was almost more than she could bear—and yet for reasons she couldn't articulate to herself she was reluctant to leave, although she knew she should.

'Alex, we can't reach any higher.'

Saffron's voice drew her attention back to her surroundings and, shaking off her thoughts, Alex slid to her feet. It was Christmas and she was home again. It might be temporary, but Finn was right. She did need closure—and she also needed to remember the good times. Like the many evenings spent in this room with Mrs Atkinson and Finn. Preparing for Christmas with the scent of spice in the air as she and Finn decorated their own tree.

'Okay. But if I am going to help with a Christmas tree then you know what we need?'

Both girls stared at her wide-eyed and Alex brandished her phone. 'Christmas music, that's what.'

She searched through her library until she found the playlist Amber had shared with them all on the morning of the first of December. A playlist she had barely glanced at, let alone played. She hit the button.

As Mariah began to tell them what she wanted for Christmas, Alex stepped over to the tree and held out her hand for an ornament. 'This is your tree, girls, so you tell me where you want things to go. Okay?'

'Okay!' Scarlett handed her a delicate silver pinecone and stared solemnly at the tree. 'I want that to go there.'

She pointed at a spot near Alex's ear, and equally solemnly, with ceremonial care, Alex hooked the shining ornament onto the branch.

''You've done a great job so far.'

Alex stood back and surveyed her handiwork before scanning the opulently decorated tree, laden with delicate baubles and ornaments in every colour and style imaginable. A crystal reindeer hung next to a jolly carved wooden snowman, and a pottery Father Christmas beamed at a gold angel. It was as far from the stylised, professionally decorated tree in the ballroom as possible. It was perfect.

She held out her hand. 'You guys have quite the collection. Next.'

'They're all Uncle Finn's. He always brings us new ones, wherever he goes. Oh, my favourite!' Saffy said, clapping her hands together before reverentially picking up a small wooden box and opening it.

Nestled inside was a perfect red glass apple. Alex caught her breath. Finn still had it all these years later.

'Oh…' Scarlett's lip wobbled as she scanned the bottom of the box. 'Look, Saffy, we're almost done and there's still the whole top of the tree to do. We haven't got enough.'

Alex palmed the small red apple, feeling the cool glass against her skin and cringing for her fifteen-year-old self—of all the things to buy the seventeen-year-old boy you had a crush on. She'd almost died of embarrassment when she handed it over and saw the hastily hidden surprise on his face. She should have bought him a T-shirt or a Yankees hat—but, no, she'd bought him an ornament. Yet he still had it. And all the others she'd picked up over the next two years. Had them and had added to them.

'Don't worry, Scarlett, a place like Blakeley Castle has lots of hidden treasure. Wait here. I bet we can finish this tree off perfectly.'

Finn pushed the door open with his shoulder, balancing the tray carefully. Mrs Atkinson would approve; the crisps and nuts were in glass bowls. He set the tray down and picked up a glass of wine before realising that Alex was nowhere to be seen. Had she slipped away? Had he pushed too hard?

'Has Alex gone?' He made the question as light as possible, as if the answer barely concerned him. The last thing he wanted was for the girls to realise there was anything wrong. 'Is that music yours? I didn't know you two liked The Pogues.' It was great that they had such good taste, but he didn't think this song was entirely suitable.

'What's a Pogue?' Scarlett asked, wandering over to lean on his leg, one small hand straying towards the bowl of crisps.

Saffron looked up from the ornament she was examining. 'Alex has gone to look for treasure.'

'For treasure?'

'For the tree. We ran out of ornaments.'

'We did go for the biggest tree we could find. I suppose it was always a possibility.'

Finn suppressed a smile as he walked over to admire the tree. The bottom two-thirds was so full of decorations there was barely a patch of green to be found, but the top third was all bare branches, with just one silver cone and a solitary red apple. He reached one finger out and sent the apple spinning.

'Okay, who wants to excavate some treasure?'

Alex backed into the room, her arms full with a large, dusty cardboard box, and Finn hastily stepped over to her, relieving her of the box.

'Thanks. It's not heavy, but it is large.'

'Where did you find that?' Saffron asked.

Alex smiled. 'I followed the clues to the attic. Now, shall we see what's inside?'

Carefully the girls lifted the lid and peered inside.

'Ornaments!' Scarlett yelled. 'Look!'

But Saffron just looked at Alex, her forehead pinched suspiciously. 'How did you know where to find them?'

'I've been here before,' Alex said. 'A long time ago. It's okay, Saffron. Your Uncle Finn owns everything in the castle. You can use these. I think the former owner would be very happy to see them hung on a tree again.'

Saffron considered Alex's words for one long moment and then she nodded. A second later she was on her hands and knees beside Scarlett, unpacking the treasures and laying them out on the coffee table.

Thank you, Finn mouthed at Alex, unsure whether he was thanking her for reassuring Saffron, getting the ornaments or just for being there.

'Look!' Scarlett held up a red glass apple. 'It's the twin of yours, Uncle Finn.'

'And so is this angel!'

'And this reindeer.'

'Don't forget I lived here before,' Finn said, his gaze not leaving Alex's.

He couldn't have looked away if he'd wanted to, and the air crackled as he watched her. Her hair had tumbled out of its usual smooth knot and her cheeks were flushed, her eyes soft.

Neither girl found his answer odd, although it didn't really make any sense, and continued to sort the ornaments.

'Here.' He handed Alex one of the glasses and she accepted it.

'Thank you. I can't believe it's got dark already. I used to like the lead-up to Christmas, the dark evenings, but now I'm just holding out for spring.'

'You don't like Christmas?' Scarlett stopped in the middle of unwrapping an ornament, her mouth a perfect O of surprise.

'It's not that I don't *like* it,' Alex reassured her. 'But my Christmases are very quiet.'

'You'll have to come to my school play,' Scarlett told her. 'We're doing it here on Christmas Eve and then singing carols— aren't we, Uncle Finn? I'm a lamb and Saffy is the narrator, which is a really big part. Bigger than Mary, whatever Polly Myers says.'

The last place Alex wanted to spend Christmas was Blakeley, but she forced a smile. 'I need to get back on Christmas Eve. My friend is waiting for me, and we always spend Christmas together.'

'Invite your friend,' Saffy suggested.

'I'll see. We were thinking of going away for Christmas, so it depends on our flights. But thank you. The party sounds amazing and I bet you two will be excellent.'

'Going away for Christmas?' Scarlett looked up from the box. 'Won't your family be sad?'

'Okay,' Finn interjected. 'Stop cross-examining Alex. Come on, step to it. More tree decorating, less chat. Someone pass me a reindeer.'

Over the next ten minutes Finn finished the tree, after arbitrating a short but fierce quarrel about whether to use tinsel or garlands—a squabble resolved by Alex declaring that she liked both.

'Okay,' he said at last. 'I think we're done here. What do you guys think? No?' His nieces were adamantly shaking their heads. 'We're not finished? What have I forgotten? Can't be the apple...we have two this year. Can't be the tinsel... Scarlett took care of that. Definitely isn't the chocolate because I sorted that...'

'The star!' Scarlett burst out. 'We haven't done the star.'

'The what?'

'The *star*!' Both yelled at once and he covered his ears.

'I think Father Christmas could probably hear that all the way in the North Pole,' he said feelingly. 'Okay. You know the drill. Out!'

Finn sensed Alex watching him as he ushered the girls out of the room. She'd curled up on the sofa, glass of wine in hand. She was contributing little to the conversation, but seemed contented, more relaxed than he'd seen her all week. It was partly the casual weekend clothes—the red sweater dress matched with grey tights and boots, the chunky silver necklace round her neck—and partly the way her smile finally reached her eyes. Maybe it was also partly the way the girls had pulled her into their circle, disarming her defences.

And possibly...probably...the talk they'd had earlier had helped. It had certainly made her presence easier for him, the long overdue clearing of the air, the explaining of misconceptions. The only problem was that without that barrier between them he was remembering all the reasons he'd failed to stay away from her all those years before. Not just her beauty but her empathy, her warm wit. The way she had seemed instinctively to know him better than anyone else. And even now her perceptive glances warmed him through.

Finn had to face the truth: Alex was the only woman he'd ever loved. But that knowledge changed nothing, because in the end she'd walked away.

He needed to remember that. Needed to remember that the girls needed stability. They only had him. Alex had made her choice long ago, and that choice had been to believe the worst of him. Even if she was still interested, even if he wanted to rekindle what they'd had, he couldn't allow anyone with so little faith near his already damaged nieces. Particularly as they both seemed to have taken to her— even the usually wary Saffron.

'Pass me the star,' he said, and Alex un- curled herself, picking up the finely wrought glittering silver star and walking over to hand it to him.

'You're doing a Mrs Atkinson!' Her smile lit up her whole face. 'Oh, how I remember the utter deliciousness of the anticipation, waiting outside, desperate to peek, knowing when I came in the tree would be lit and the star on the top. I think of it every Christmas.'

'You should go and see her. She would love to see you.'

'And I would love to see her. I couldn't be- fore, I didn't want to be anywhere near Blake- ley, but maybe now it might be easier.' She pushed his shoulder impatiently. 'Go on, put the tree lights on! I'll switch the main lights off and let the girls back in before they com- bust.'

Finn obeyed, after making sure the star was straight. The tree lights sprang to life, flickering more brightly as Alex dimmed the overhead lights. She stood silhouetted by the door and Finn had a sudden vision of how his

life might have been if she'd believed in him
all those years ago…if she'd allowed him to
support her through the fallout of her parents'
fall from grace.

But that life had disappeared as surely as
Lola. All that could ever be was a friendship
of sorts. It was all he could risk for the sake
of his girls.

CHAPTER EIGHT

ALEX HAD NO idea why people complained about Monday morning. She *liked* Mondays. Too often there was so little purpose to the weekend. She'd clean, run, do some dutiful yoga, maybe cook, occasionally see a film or see a play, but it was all just killing time until Monday, when she could fill her mind and her time with work, reminding herself that she had a purpose, that she was good at what she did. It helped that she worked in public relations and had a legitimate interest in checking her emails and social media channels throughout the weekend, never switching off her phone.

Her life might seem small to some, but it was the life she wanted, the life she'd chosen. Just as she'd chosen London, cacophonous and dirty and full of people. The city surrounded her, protected her. No one saw her there. She was hidden in plain sight, able to sleepwalk through her life untouching and untouched.

Which meant she'd better be careful not to spend too many more cosy evenings with Finn and his cute-as-a-button nieces. There had been moments on Saturday evening when his dark-eyed gaze had rested on her for just a second too long...moments when she'd been über-aware of his every movement...moments when she'd been fixated on the vee of his throat exposed by his shirt, his wrists, the nape of his neck, all those soft, vulnerable spots in such a hard, fit body. A body she'd once had the freedom to love and to explore. The only body she'd ever...

No. She wasn't going there. She couldn't. It didn't matter that Finn hadn't sold those photos—maybe deep down she had always known he wasn't capable of such cruelty. What did matter was that she'd made herself vulnerable and it had backfired spectacularly. She could never allow that to happen again.

With renewed energy, Alex returned her focus to her laptop and the social media plans she'd been reviewing, pausing only to scribble notes and thoughts, the coffee Kaitlin had brought her cooling at her elbow. When she finally looked up the weak winter morning sun had disappeared and the sky had turned an ominous yellowy grey, the clouds low and heavy. A snow sky if ever she had seen one.

The air shifted and Alex knew Finn had walked into the office. She didn't need to look and check if she was right. A sixth sense had shivered through her body, every nerve awake.

'Okay, everyone,' he said. He didn't need to raise his voice. It was clear and commanding it reached every corner of the room. 'The forecast is for snow, and lots of it, so the minibus is waiting outside for those of you who live in Reading and London. I suggest you take work home with you. It may be a couple of days before the roads are passable. I remember being snowed in for a week when I was a boy.'

Alex couldn't stop herself from looking up as he finished speaking, knowing the exact week he was referring to. He was looking directly at her, and their eyes held for what seemed like an eternity as they were caught in their own private world of memories.

It wasn't until someone claimed Finn's attention that she was recalled to her surroundings. Cheeks hot, she checked to make sure no one had noticed their momentary lapse, but everyone was too busy talking about the snow to have paid her any attention.

'Alex?'

Finn strolled over to her desk and she willed her cheeks to cool. 'Hi.'

'I'm aware that you won't have anything suitable for snow with you. I could send you back to London...'

Yes! That would be perfect, and give her exactly the breathing space she needed. So why wasn't she jumping up at his words and grabbing her laptop?

'But if you'd rather ride out the weather here then of course you may,' he continued. 'I can't see the snow lasting too long, and if you do want to stay then I can kit you out. Time you started living the brand.'

Oh, that smile! The way it lit his whole face, turning a slightly aloof handsomeness into something much warmer—and so much more dangerous.

'I'd better stay,' she said, only a little reluctantly. 'There's a lot to do and there's something I want to discuss with you. Work,' she added.

'Of course,' he said lightly. 'What else could it be?'

'Exactly.'

'Give me fifteen minutes to sort everything out and then I'll be right with you.'

'Fine.'

She didn't mean to be so curt, but there were so many things unsaid, so many things she was scared of saying. So many things best left in the past where they belonged.

Alex stayed at her desk as the rest of the staff gathered their belongings, most of them about to leave. She scrolled through various social media feeds, adding notes when something caught her eye, gradually falling back into the absorbed spell of the world she preferred. A world where noise dimmed and people faded and all she knew was her work.

After a few minutes she looked up, aware that the very atmosphere of the room had changed again. It was no surprise when she looked around to see that the office had emptied and there was just Finn, leaning against the wall, watching her.

'You look busy.'

'That's what you're paying me for.'

'So busy that you haven't even noticed the snow?'

He nodded towards the window and Alex turned and stared at the view. The grass had already been covered with a fine dusting of snow, but judging by the big, fat flakes floating down from the sky in ever-increasing spirals it wouldn't be long before the snow was ankle-deep.

'Time to get you some boots. Come on.'

Closing her laptop, Alex followed him down the back stairs. His stockroom was in the old tack room at the back of the stables. It was almost unrecognisable, the rough wood panelling sanded and painted, the tack pegs replaced with neat shelves, the dirt floor covered in grey tiles. Each shelf was filled with folded clothes, labelled by size and type.

'All employees have a generous clothes allowance,' Finn explained as he ushered her in. 'They need to believe in us, live our values and look the part. Hawk isn't just spin and fancy campaigns, it's a way of life. Here, try these.' He held out a pair of sturdy yet oddly elegant leather boots. 'They're lined, waterproofed, and the sole has been especially designed for icy conditions.'

He eyed her up and down in a way that was purely professional and yet still made her feel exposed. She resisted the urge to wrap her arms around herself.

'Okay, and try this, these, this and…let me see…this.'

'So when you say "live the brand", you mean be kitted out from head to toe?' She took the grey trousers and the white shirt, the berry-red fleecy jumper and black down jacket from him. 'I hate to break it to you but

I'm a city girl. There's not much use for waterproof trousers in Chelsea.'

'You're back in the country today and you'll be glad to have those trousers by this evening. Try them. They might surprise you. Our Chiltern range combines cutting-edge technology and fabrics with design-led style. And even Chelsea girls need warm hands and feet.' He added socks, gloves and a hat to the pile. 'You know, there's something I've been meaning to ask you since last week…'

'Oh?'

Alex's heart began to hammer, with strong, painful thuds. There had been enough treading old ground at the weekend. She needed to concentrate on moving forward. Being back at Blakeley, spending all this time with Finn, was dangerous. It was reminding her of all she'd used to be, all she'd used to want. They had to get their relationship back on purely professional ground before it was too late.

'Is your agency really called the Happy Ever After Agency? That's its actual name?'

That was his burning question? Alex didn't know whether to laugh or sigh in relief. 'I know. It's unusual, whimsical in some ways, but that was our purpose. We wanted to stand out.'

'You've managed that.'

Alex shifted, balancing the pile of clothes more securely. 'It has a dual meaning. Obviously we want all our clients to have complete peace of mind, and to know that using us means there will always be a successful outcome. But at the same time it's a personal wish. Once none of us had the security we wanted; our futures felt unsure. The agency was our way of taking back control. It's our happy-ever-after.'

Alex looked up and saw such utter comprehension in Finn's eyes it almost undid her. It was as if she were naked in front of him.

She smiled awkwardly. 'Thanks for these, but I'd better get back to work. Let me know when you're ready to have that talk.'

But as she left the room, Finn fell into step beside her.

'There are four of you, aren't there? I did my research before employing you. Obviously the Armarian royal ball was a huge coup, but I needed to know that such a new agency was capable of handling my work. And I have to tell you, Alex, I was impressed. Not only do you have lots of glowing testimonials, but you've also managed to make one archduke very happy. And apparently there's another equally happy billionaire—Deangelo Santos? Not bad work for just eight months in existence.'

Alex couldn't see his expression, but the teasing note in his voice was enough to raise her defensive hackles. 'You're right, our testimonials *are* impressive. And that's because we work dammed hard to make them that way. As for the rest, the love lives of my business partners are really none of your business. What's important is that we offer exemplary service for everyone, whether they are an archduke or a local café wanting some social media advice.'

'As I said, glowing testimonials.' He paused, and when he spoke again there was a curious tension in his voice. 'So how did you end up in Chelsea? Did you stay in touch with your godmother? I often wondered if that was where you went. The two of you were pretty close, I remember. I did try her a few times, but she wouldn't speak to me. It makes sense if you were living there, I suppose.'

They'd reached the top of the stairs and Alex dropped the pile of clothes onto the nearest desk. 'What does it matter, Finn? It's history. None of it is relevant to why I'm here and the job I'm here to do.'

He didn't answer at first, running a hand through his dark hair, expression unreadable. When had he achieved that inscrutability? She'd always been able to read him before.

Shame engulfed her. She should have read him when he'd told her he hadn't sold those photos, should have seen his innocence in his eyes then.

'It matters because I let you down,' he said at last, his voice hoarse. 'You needed me and I let you down. That's why I need to know what happened to you back then. Why I need to know that you were safe and happy. That you fled to your godmother's and were looked after and loved. I need to know that, Alex. Because I failed you. That's why I wanted you back here at Blakeley. I needed to know that you're okay. And I don't think you are, are you?'

The silence was absolute. Just the two of them stood there in the large, cavernous space, his words echoing around them. Alex was still, staring at him, wonder and fear warring in her expression.

'You don't need to worry about me. Not then, and not now,' she said at last.

'That's nonsense. We were best friends. You gave me your virginity, Alex, and I gave you my heart. I loved you, and I think you loved me. And then your life fell apart and I just watched it happen.'

Her mouth quivered. 'You were twenty.'

'I was old enough to do more. Do something.' He should have held on to her, should have offered her refuge and the unconditional love she had needed. But he'd failed her, utterly and completely. 'I let you drive me away because you hurt my pride. What kind of man did that make me? *Does* it make me?'

At that, her eyes softened. 'You were always the proudest boy. You would never accept help with anything. I should have trusted you, Finn.'

She touched his cheek: a fleeting caress, burning through him.

'Never question what kind of man you are. Look at your girls, look at the village—I never knew it so prosperous. And look at this office, full of people willing to move their lives for you and your vision. You're a better man than I ever deserved.'

'Tell me what happened.' It was as much command as plea. 'Tell me where you've been.'

She regarded him for a long few seconds then sighed, a deep shuddering sigh that seemed to come from her soul. 'I don't talk about it, Finn. I try not to even think about it. It's buried deep inside. It has to be. It's the only way I can keep going. But you are right. You of all people deserve the truth. But not here. I need some air, need to breathe properly if I am going to do this.'

Finn glanced out at the still whirling snow, now ankle-deep on the ground, then nodded at the pile of clothes on the desk. 'In that case it's time you got branded up.'

It took Alex less than five minutes to change, and when she returned to the office she was outdoors-ready, the dark trousers showcasing long, lean legs, the berry-red top just visible under the half-zipped jacket. She'd already laced up her boots, and as she reached him she put on her hat before slipping her hands into the gloves.

'You should be on the front cover of our catalogue!' he said.

He was only half joking, but she shook her head.

'My modelling days are well and truly over. I never enjoyed it, but my mother loved it. Loved people saying I reminded them of her. It was something that bonded us. And I needed that.'

'Do you still see her?'

Her gaze fell, but not before he saw the dark shadows in her eyes. 'She prefers not to be reminded of that time.'

There wasn't anything anyone could say to that and Finn didn't try. 'Come on, let's try out those boots. They're a new model, not due for release until later next year.'

The cold hit them as soon as they stepped outside, fresh and icy, momentarily robbing Finn of his breath. By unspoken accord they walked away from the castle and away from the lake, to the parkland at the back of the castle. It was now officially open for business, with nature trails and hikes winding through, a treetop walk newly installed, bike tracks freshly laid, but he was sure they'd have it to themselves. The weather was bound to deter all but the most hardened of adventurers, and the snow was swirling more quickly now, blocking visibility.

'You know, these jackets are designed for proper alpine conditions. I didn't think they could be tested so close to home.'

Finn turned to look at Alex as he spoke, blinking the snow out of his eyes. She was transformed, cheeks pink with cold, the snow coating her with white glitter, her smile wide and genuine.

'This is bracing!'

'That's one word for it. I was about to call in the huskies.'

It was easier to walk and talk now they

were in the woods. The snow was slowed by the branches overhead, and the trees sheltered them from the worst of the wind. Alex looked so much more relaxed, arms swinging as she tramped through the snow, that Finn almost wanted to forget the purpose of the walk and just let her have this time. But he knew getting her to open up was hard, that this chance might never come again, and the curiosity and renewed regret which had hit him so hard in Armaria needed answers.

He had to move on. Once and for all.

'So,' he said, as lightly as he could. 'Tell me about your transformation from Lola Beaumont to Alexandra Davenport.'

Her smile instantly dimmed, as though it had never been. 'First I need you to tell me something. If Penelope hadn't had to stop working so suddenly, would you ever have told me that you'd found me? Or after looking me up and researching my agency would you have just walked away and forgotten about me again?'

'I never forgot about you, ever. But as for the rest…? I don't know,' Finn confessed, 'I told myself to leave the past where it was. The girls need me now, so what's the point of dragging up the past? But, Alex, seeing you again was like rediscovering part of myself I didn't know I had lost. I picked up the phone to call the agency time after time, only to realise I didn't know what to say. I wrote dozens of emails I couldn't send. When I finally actually had a genuine reason to call you I don't know if I was more relieved or disappointed when Amber answered instead of you. It was clear Amber had no idea where Blakeley was or what it meant to you. When I said we needed you urgently and offered to send a car for you, she agreed. But it wasn't her agreement I should have sought. It was yours. I'm sorry. I shouldn't have blindsided you the way I did, insisting you came straight here. I shouldn't have threatened you to make you stay. I just didn't want you to leave without knowing that you were okay. That you were happy. *Are* you happy, Alex?'

It was the most important question of all.

'I'm content.'

'And that's enough?'

She shrugged. 'It has to be.'

'I don't believe you,' he said roughly. 'The girl I knew would never settle for "content".'

'That girl is gone. You need to accept that, Finn. Lola Beaumont has gone.'

'No.'

He stopped and turned to face her, holding her loosely by the shoulders. She made no attempt to break free, just stood there, her eyes entreating him. To what? To stop pushing? To let her stay in the dream world she inhabited? The one where she told herself she needed nothing and no one and 'content' was as good as it got?

Maybe it would be kinder to leave her there, to let her sleepwalk through the rest of her life. But didn't he owe it to the girl he'd loved, that sweet and sassy and misunderstood wild child, to help her live again? Because, painful and unpredictable as life could be, it was better than barely living at all.

He couldn't make that decision for her. No one could. But he could help her.

'Lola Beaumont was always a chameleon,' he said. 'Maybe that's why it was so easy for you to leave her behind. Because half the time she was just a costume. You modelled her just as much as you modelled any of those designer outfits and perfumes. But there was always far more to you than that costume. I knew it. Mrs Atkinson knew it. Hell, half the village knew it. I'd say that the only person who didn't know it was you. You fooled your parents and your teachers, and most of those toffee-nosed friends of yours, but you didn't fool me then and you don't fool me now. You can call yourself Lola or Alex or Jane, for all

I care. But I still see you. And you are worth seeing. You always were.'

Alex didn't answer. She just stood, mute and compliant under his grasp, her eyes swimming with unshed tears.

The tension stretched until he could bear it no longer. He'd promised himself not to get involved, reminded himself that there was no future here, that the girls came first. But the girls were at school and the future seemed like a distant dream as he looked deep into the ocean of Alex's eyes, no longer pebbles but deep, deep grey and full of passion, suppressed and hidden, but there. He knew it, he saw it, it called to him, and his blood thrilled to it.

With a muttered curse he threw his promises and scruples aside and bent to her.

His kiss was neither gentle nor exploratory, but a deep claiming that sent his blood dancing. Her mouth was warm under his, welcoming him even as she made no move to touch him, to close the distance between them. Emboldened, Finn deepened the kiss, his hands still light upon her, feeling the delicacy of her bones beneath the tips of his fingers.

'No.'

The word sent him reeling back. Had he misread the situation? Misread *her*? Surely she'd come alive under his kiss? Or was that merely wishful thinking on his part?

'No,' she said again. 'You wanted a story and I promised you one. You need to understand who I am now, Finn. And then you'll know. I'm not a chameleon. I'm just empty. I always was.'

CHAPTER NINE

Finn glanced at Alex but she stared straight ahead, her mouth set. There was no trace of the warm, yielding woman in the granite hardness of her face, and her eyes were now like stone. What did she think she could tell him that he didn't know? He knew her truth. Had tasted it and loved it and yearned for it. But he had asked for her story and she was ready to tell him. He owed her the listening.

They hadn't discussed their path, but they didn't need to. There was only one destination, and as they tramped through the still, snow-decked woods it seemed to Finn that, despite Alex's desperate words, her past wasn't as done and dusted as she claimed. How could it be when she knew her way better than he?

Finally, a small cottage came into view, chimney first, and then the rest, curious and crooked, more like something out of a fairy-tale than a real, live cottage.

'You haven't let this out as well.'

It wasn't a question.

'No.' Finn deliberately kept his voice low and his tone matter-of-fact, as if the kiss had never happened, not wanting to scare her. 'It's too impractical all the way out here. Hard for people to get to, too much of a trek for regular cleaning. Besides…' his voice was so low he wasn't sure she heard it '… I didn't want anyone else here.'

She didn't respond. Finn couldn't tell if her heightened colour was due to his words and the memories they evoked, or simply a reaction to the biting cold.

He had the key to the front door in his pocket and she slanted a sideways glance at him as he produced it. 'How very Boy Scout of you. How did you know we were coming here?'

'I always carry it,' he said.

The key stayed on his key ring, the original from before. It was a talisman, a symbol, even more than the key to the castle. That one symbolised his change in status. This key symbolised the moment he had truly found what he wanted. The moment he had lost it.

He opened the door and stood aside to let Alex enter. No one knew when the cottage had been built or who had originally lived there. Right in the middle of the woods, with no garden separating it from the trees around, the stone-built old cottage looked as if it belonged on a film set.

The front door led straight into the one original room, a kitchen and living space, dominated by a wood-burning stove which heated both the radiators and the hot water. A later addition housed the downstairs bathroom and scullery; upstairs was just one large bedroom.

'It's been redecorated.' Alex stood stock-still, her keen gaze taking in every detail.

Finn went over to the stove and began to load it with logs from the filled basket. 'One of the first things I had done when I first bought the castle. It didn't need much; structurally it was surprisingly sound, and the damp was because of the lack of regular heating rather than anything more sinister. A damp-proof course, new plastering and painting and a deep clean and it's perfectly habitable, if a little rustic. I come here sometimes when I need time alone, to think. There's always someone who needs me at the castle or in the office, always decisions to make. I built the business on creativity and sometimes I feel that slipping away. Do you mind? Me using it?'

Her eyebrows arched in elegant if disingenuous surprise. 'Why would I?'

'Because this was your special place.'

'No.' Now it was her turn to be almost inaudible. 'It was ours.'

It didn't take long to light the stove. Alex had taken off her boots and curled up in one of the armchairs, pulled close to benefit from the stove's heat. Finn sat opposite her. He'd come out determined to get answers, closure, and yet he still felt as if he were fighting through thickets to reach her. She was as hidden as ever, only her momentary loss of control in the woods hinting that she was reachable if he just kept pushing.

The stove always heated quickly, and within a few minutes it was warm enough to cast their coats to one side. Alex didn't speak for a long time and Finn sat back, letting her set the pace. It was surprisingly soothing, just sitting, watching the emotions play out on her face. She wasn't as in control as she would have him believe.

Finally, she sighed and turned to him, curling up tighter in the chair as if, like a hedgehog, the curve of her body would protect her. 'What are you doing, Finn?'

'I was about to offer you tea. We might have biscuits somewhere too.'

'Not right now. I mean, why are you here, at Blakeley? You could have made a new life for you and the girls anywhere. Why exhume all these ghosts? Why are we right here, right now?'

It was a good question. One he had asked himself several times whilst negotiating a price for the castle and estate and beginning the extensive renovations and investment: an investment that had made a serious dent in the fortune he had so painstakingly built up.

He stared at the polished stove, at the room with its scrubbed table, the comfy armchairs, the bookshelves. He was a thirty-year-old man and the retreat he had refurbished for himself was no man cave. Instead it was an exercise in nostalgia. Because this had been Lola's place. In those days the armchairs had needed reupholstering, the cottage had often been damp and cold, covered in dust and cobwebs, but to them it had been playhouse, palace and freedom.

When she'd been sent to boarding school she'd solemnly presented him with the key—the key he still carried—knowing he needed a sanctuary, away from his father's anger and his sister's unhappiness.

And this was where they had slipped away, nearly ten years ago to the day, on the night of her eighteenth birthday. Memory of that night was in every line of her defensive body.

'Blakeley is my home. It always was. I wanted the girls to grow up here, free and wild and safe. The childhood we so nearly had? I want that for them.'

She nodded, as if she had anticipated his answer.

'Okay.'

She was tense now, ramrod-straight in the armchair as if she was being interrogated. Her hair had slipped out of its coil while she wore the hat and she had pulled it back into a tight ponytail which accentuated the taut lines of her face and her high, haughty cheekbones. She wore the berry-red fleece as if it were cashmere. Still every inch the lady of the manor.

'What do you want to know?'

'Everything.'

She huffed out a laugh. 'You don't ask for much, do you?'

She looked down at her hands, and when she spoke again it was as if she were telling a story.

'No one knows this, Finn. Not even Harriet or Amber or Emilia. Sometimes even I don't know it. Lola belongs to a different time, a different place. She's a story. A fairy-tale or a cautionary tale.'

He didn't argue, not this time. 'How does it start?'

She smiled, a mechanical curve of her mouth with no life or joy in it. 'How does any fairy-tale start? Once upon a time there was a little girl who thought she was a princess. She lived in a beautiful castle and had everything she wanted: an antique dolls' house, a rocking horse, a real horse. She was spoiled and fêted and allowed to roam free and no one was as exciting or as glamorous as her parents. Everywhere they went people took photos of them, and everyone told the little girl how very lucky she was. And the little girl believed it.'

Finn inhaled, desperate to pull her into his arms and kiss the brittleness away, but he held himself still. 'Go on.'

'Sometimes her mummy and daddy seemed to forget about the Princess, and sometimes it seemed like they only liked her if she was wild and beautiful and fun. But she knew that it must be her fault when they forgot her or were impatient, because her parents were perfect, so she made sure she was always wild and free and beautiful. Sometimes it got her in trouble, but her parents didn't mind. They liked it that way.'

It was almost unbearable, listening to her

recite the facts of her life in an almost sing-song fashion, but again Finn restrained himself from interrupting. He'd asked, demanded to bear witness. He had to follow through.

'The Princess had one true friend, and when she grew up she knew he was her one true love. And so, on her eighteenth birthday, she sneaked out of her party to be with him. That was the last time she was truly happy. Because that night a curse hit her family, and by the end of the week her father was disgraced and dead and her mother had run away. Neither of them remembered the Princess. Not even in their goodbye notes…'

She paused, her throat working, and Finn's fists tightened, his need to give her comfort more acute than ever.

'No one wanted the Princess to be wild and free and beautiful any more. They wanted her to be humiliated—and she was. Unbearably so. It was like being poisoned. Every part of her hurt. Everything she touched shattered, people turned away from her, and she thought the boy she loved had betrayed her. She didn't know how to carry on. For a while she didn't. She just lay there and hoped it was all a bad dream.'

'Alex…'

'For a long time she thought she was broken. She had ended up by the sea, staying in a cottage in a place where no one knew her. There she decided to stop being a princess. She changed her name and used the little bit of money her father hadn't embezzled and the bailiffs couldn't claim to go back to college and get the qualifications she'd been too wild and free to bother with before. And she decided she was never going to let anyone else tell her story again. She was going to be the one who decided how her story was told and she got a job that helped her do that. No one knew she used to be a princess and that was just how she liked it. And she lived quietly ever after and that was how she liked it too.'

She lapsed into silence, almost unbearably still. None of the tale was new. He'd lived it with her. She'd touched on aspects of it over the last week. But to hear her tell it with so little emotion gave her words a power he hadn't imagined. Finally, he understood how broken she had been. How broken she still was, for all her protestations, and he ached to fix her.

'Where did you go to college? Did you live with your godmother?'

She blinked and the spell dissolved. 'Finn, since I left Blakeley I've worked for everything I've achieved the old-fashioned way. No trading off my name or connections. No trust fund, obviously. The debt collectors took care of that. No home, no contacts—I only saw my godmother a couple of times; she was as keen to disassociate herself from the Beaumonts as everyone else. When I found out that she had left me her house I was shocked. To be honest I almost didn't accept it. I didn't want anything from before. But it wasn't just my life the inheritance would change. We'd been planning the agency for a couple of years, my co-partners and I, and I knew I could give the others the home and stability they needed.'

'And you? Has it given you what you need?'

Her smile was brittle. 'Come on, Finn. You know as well as I do that stability is an illusion and there really is no place to call home.'

'You used to pretend this was your home.'

'That's all any of it was. Pretence. I wasn't the girl my parents wanted me to be, they weren't the great love story they told the world they were, the fortune we spent wasn't ours to spend. Everything I was and everything I knew was a lie. That's my truth.'

'Not everything.'

'Everything,' she whispered, and her eyes filled with tears.

He'd wanted real emotion and here it was, raw and painful. 'We were real. That night was real.'

But she shook her head. 'No. That night was as much an illusion as the rest. It was cursed, like everything else. Those photos plastered everywhere…me plastered everywhere…something sweet and sacred and special reduced to sniggers and scandal. The things I said to you. Accused you of. Believed. If it had been real how could I have said those things?'

'It was real,' he repeated. 'The most real thing that has ever happened to me. You want to know why I came back here? Because this is where I was most alive. I have skied down deadly slopes and climbed mountains and kayaked through rapids and seen some of the most sacred and ancient sights in the world, and not once have I felt the way I felt that night. As if I finally understood my place in the universe. And I let that go. I let you go.'

'I shouldn't have come here; you shouldn't have brought me here. I can't do this, Finn. Not now.' She jumped to her feet and rushed to the door, the tears falling freely now. 'You should have let me stay gone.'

'Alex.' It took three strides to reach her, seconds to touch her, to hold her once again, to pull her in close. 'I'm sorry. But I'm here now. Let me in, Alex. Let me in.'

* * *

It was too much. The past was all around her. No matter how hard she worked, no matter how far she ran, no matter how much she buried herself, it wasn't enough. She would never be free of the curse.

But strong arms were around her, pulling her in close. Finn's scent enveloped her, warm and spicy and safe. The low burr of his voice vibrated through her as he murmured words of comfort, of reassurance.

For ten years she had stood alone, needing no one, trusting no one, wanting no one. No dates, no relationships, no one-night stands. Just work and purpose and desperately trying to appease whatever malevolent spirit had taken her world and destroyed it, freezing her in pain and loneliness.

She sometimes thought that if she hadn't met Harriet, Emilia and Amber she just might have given up, slipped away into nothingness. Her friends anchored her, and she allowed herself to care for them—but she accepted nothing in return except some company. And she was right to do so, because Harriet and Emilia would soon be moving on, and she couldn't believe that sweet, warm hearted Amber would stay single much longer. Amber yearned for a family, and she deserved one, deserved to be loved.

And then Alex would be alone once more. She knew it, and she was prepared for it. Accepted it. At times she thought she deserved it. But right now it was hard to remember that. Hard to remember why she needed to stand alone when there was someone giving her strength and support. Someone she could lean on.

Not someone. Finn. The boy she'd loved. No longer a boy, a man. A successful man. A good man. A man with a life and commitments she couldn't imagine. Commitments whose needs superseded hers.

Slowly, reluctantly, Alex disentangled herself from Finn's clasp, blinking back still unshed tears, trying to put her mask back in place.

'Finn…'

But then she made the mistake of looking up. Looking up at a face she knew as well as her own, older, honed by life into something more than handsome, more real than the youthful good looks she'd once crushed on. At a firm mouth she knew to be capable of tenderness, dark eyes full of sympathy, yes, but more than that, blazing with heat and want. Heat and want for *her*.

It had been so long since anyone had looked at her that way. Since *he* had looked at her that way. Right here, in this cottage, when she had slipped out of her dress, feeling like a goddess seeing the awe in his eyes, like a supplicant when he had first reached out to run a finger down her arm and she had really, truly known his touch.

She'd wanted him since she was fourteen, but he'd pushed her away, the two years separating them a chasm. But at eighteen she'd been an adult, and he had been powerless to resist her any longer. And she'd never been able to resist him. So how could she now?

'Finn…' she repeated, but this time it was a plea. For him to let her go or to hold her tighter? She barely knew herself.

But it didn't matter, because he took it as an invitation. Strong hands cupped her face, fingers burning into her cheeks, branding her, claiming her, as he searched her face. She had no idea what he was looking for or what she was showing him, but whatever it was he seemed satisfied. A wolfish smile spread slowly over his face, his eyes heating even more until she was dizzy with the want slowly filling her, warming her, bringing her back to life.

'Finn,' she said again, and this time it was

all plea. A plea for something, anything, to happen. She couldn't take the anticipation any longer. It was twisting her stomach, making her pulse pound through her body, a rhythm of need.

'Welcome back,' he said softly, and bent his head to hers.

The moment their mouths met the years rolled back and she was once again an eighteen-year-old in the fierce grip of first love. His kiss was as firm and as sure, as overwhelming, and she melted into it, into him. And, as she'd known he would, he caught her, his grip solid and real. That kiss in the woods had been one of pity, of solace. This was a kiss filled with desire. And she succumbed to it. All the reasons, the *good* reasons, to pull away had flown. There were no thoughts. Her head was blessedly empty of anything but him.

Slowly, skilfully, he increased the pressure, and her mouth opened to him greedily. Heated back to life, back to action, Alex wound her arms around his neck, angling herself until she could deepen the kiss, her hands gripping the sensitive skin at his nape, pulling him into her. Desperately she moved closer, until every inch of her was pressed to every inch of him, ten years of suppressed need and desire and want spilling out of her. It wasn't close enough.

Finally, finally, his hands slipped from her shoulders, travelling with devastating slowness down her ribcage, caressing the curve of her breasts until they came to rest momentarily at her waist. His mouth left hers to skim butterfly kisses along her jaw, down to her neck, and she tilted her head to allow him access, shivering at his languorous journey.

Couldn't he feel her burning up? She didn't want a slow, sweet seduction. She wanted hard and fast and right now, please. To feel and to live.

Impatient, she wriggled even closer, taking a moment to enjoy his tortured groan before slipping one hand down to where his shirt met his trousers, allowing it to explore the hard planes of his stomach, before dipping it lower to the waistband.

He groaned again. 'Alex. Not so fast.'

'Why? Why wait?' She pulled back to examine him, confused. Didn't he want this? It certainly felt as if he did.

'I've waited ten years to do this again,' he said with a crooked smile. 'I want to savour every minute.'

'But,' she pointed out, 'we could do it fast, and then start again and do it slow.'

His eyes flared and her stomach quivered at the look in them, as if he wanted to devour her whole.

'I knew you were still in there somewhere,' he said, gravelly and low-voiced.

For one second Alex wanted to retreat. To deny the part of her sparking into life, hungry and eager and ready. She had been hiding this girl, this woman, for so long, afraid of what might be unleashed if she allowed her to feel and to do. But she was so tired of hiding her. She had told her story and Finn had borne witness. He had looked into her and found her, denied her emptiness and coaxed her back to life. She would not run and she would not hide. Not today.

'I want you, Finn Hawkin.' Alex spoke clearly, enunciating every syllable.

Slowly he reached out and took her hand, strong, cool fingers entwining with hers. 'I want you too. I think I have since the moment you got out of that car, all professional and cold and so damn desirable. I nearly kissed you that same evening. But you weren't ready...'

'I'm ready now. Less talk and more kissing.'

He looked at her, really looked, as if he could see beyond the practical clothes emblazoned with his trademark, could see inside her skin to her beating heart and thundering pulse and aching need.

'Yes, ma'am.'

Tugging her hand, Finn led her to the door which she knew concealed the staircase leading up to the bedroom. Last time she had led him, overcoming the last vestiges of his doubt, proving that she was grown up, a woman. Now it was him leading the way, but she had no doubts. Her blood thundered round her body as she followed him up the stairs. Home at last.

CHAPTER TEN

'WHAT ARE YOU doing?'

Alex jumped as the clear voice sang through the air, and as she did so her feet slipped in opposite directions. She yelped, desperately trying to get them back under control.

'Have you done that before?' Saffron padded through the snow to peer down at Alex's feet, strapped securely into long, slim skis.

'Believe it or not I used to be very good, but I haven't skied since I was seventeen. I'm hoping it's like riding a bike and that when you get your balance you remember how to do it.'

Alex peered down the gentle but lengthy slope which led from the very back of the formal gardens down to the fields that formed the working farm part of the estate. She'd not skied this slope since she was much younger than Saffron. It had been far too tame for her. Now she wasn't entirely sure she could get all the way down.

'Can I have a go?' Saffron looked wistfully at the skis.

Alex nodded. 'If you look in the cupboard in the boot room, you'll find some boots and skis about your size.'

'How do you know?'

'Your uncle mentioned it. There're several pairs of boots, so make sure you get your size. Go on, go and get them, and if I make it down in one piece I'll show you how I did it.'

The boots and skis were Alex's own, long since grown out of and discarded, just as this pair had been. A fraction of her old possessions, her old life, still here in the castle, reminding her of who she'd used to be.

But the memories didn't hurt the way they'd used to. Being at Blakeley didn't hurt the way she'd expected now she was starting to feel again. Instead there was a kind of peace at being here; she'd come full circle. Come home. Back to Finn.

Oh, she was no longer the besotted teenager she had been back then. She had no romantic dreams or hopes of a happy-ever-after. A few happy hours couldn't change a girl that much. Her life was in London, at the agency, building her career. Finn's was here. He had responsibilities she couldn't imagine: to his nieces, to his employees, to the village. Responsibilities she didn't have any share in and didn't want any part of. Better not to dream of any future and leave on Christmas Eve as planned.

But there were still a few days before that happened. A few days of negotiating her way around Finn.

Alex couldn't stop the smile curving her mouth, and her hands gripped the ski poles as she remembered the taste and the feel of him, the fire and heat and life. It had been five days since their tryst at the cottage. Five days since he had breathed new purpose into her. Five days since she had held and kissed him. Since he had kissed her. Since she had touched and been touched.

Because of course he lived with his nieces, so she couldn't come to the castle, and she worked for him, so he couldn't come to the cottage, and it was much better to chalk their afternoon's lovemaking up to emotion and nostalgia and aim for a mutually agreeable professional friendship. Or something.

Only… Alex had seen the way Finn looked at her when he thought she wasn't looking. And she certainly couldn't stop fixating on his wrists, his throat, the firm line of his mouth…

Their business was still unfinished. She knew it and he knew it. The knowledge gave every interaction between them a certain edge, and she couldn't help thrilling to it just as she had all those years ago, when she had sent him those photos.

Full circle, indeed. Luckily she was older and wiser now. The only photos she would be taking were for the Hawk social media accounts...

'Got them!' Saffy appeared on the path, arms laden with boots and skis. 'What do I do now?'

Alex surveyed the girl critically. 'Good, you're in waterproof trousers. That will make falling down a lot easier.' She laughed as Saffy glared. 'You *will* fall down. A lot! So, first things first. Sit on that bench...'

She pointed with her pole to a bench perched on the top of the hill, so passers-by could sit and enjoy the view in more temperate weather.

'And change your boots. Whatever you do, do not put your foot on the floor in just your socks or you are going to have icy toes. Make sure you do the boots up as tightly as possible and then give me a shout to let me know you're ready. Okay?'

She waited for Saffy's nod and then turned to face the hill again, bending her knees experimentally, tilting her body forward. It instinctively knew what to do.

'Like riding a bike,' she murmured as she pushed herself off, keeping her feet tilted slightly together to slow her down as she found her balance again. 'Oh, yes, that's the way.'

She wasn't going to win any prizes for style or speed, but Alex made it to the bottom in one piece, even turning to stop rather than exaggerating her snow plough.

She looked up to see Saffy waving enthusiastically.

'That was amazing, show me!'

'Okay,' Alex called as she began to make her way back up the slope.

This was a lot harder. She was so out of practice she couldn't help sliding about. Any grace or technique was non-existent, and she couldn't help but think longingly of the days when she hadn't even had to think, her skiing technique utterly innate, as had been her horse-riding ability, also long gone. She hadn't been near a horse since Strawberry had been sold.

'Put the skis onto the ground, one in front of each foot and close together, and put one foot into one of the bindings. It should click in. Leave the other one until I get there. Got it?'

'I think so!'

By the time Alex reached Saffron the girl

had attached one boot to a ski. Alex checked the bindings and made sure each boot was properly secure and nodded.

'Good job. Right, take my sticks and use them to balance while you put the other ski on.'

She barely remembered her own first ski lesson; she'd been on the slopes and on horseback from the moment she could walk. But she did remember the insistence on self-sufficiency. A good skier knew how to look after her own equipment.

It took Saffron a few goes, but eventually her foot was in and she stood there, wobbling like a baby duck about to take its first step.

Alex held up her phone. 'Smile! Your uncle won't want to miss this.'

She snapped the beaming face and then, as she returned her phone to a secure inside pocket, where it hopefully would survive any falls, realisation hit her. She hadn't seen such open joy in Saffy over the two weeks she'd been at Blakeley. The girl's smile was infectious, and Alex couldn't help beaming back as she instructed her.

'Okay. Shuffle forward, tiny steps…that's it…to the top of the hill. Now I want you to do what I just did: a controlled, slow glide. If you try and point your skis towards each

other it slows you. Now, bend your knees…
that's it…and let your weight shift forward.'

'It feels weird.'

'I know, and it's so tempting to lean back,
but don't! Right. The main thing is to try and
keep your balance, but don't worry if you fall.
It's inevitable. We all fall. It's how we get up
that counts. Right, on the count of three: one,
two, three.'

Alex waited until Saffron set off, in a slow,
uncertain half-glide, and followed behind her,
shouting encouragement.

'That's it. Nice and controlled. Lovely! Oh,
well done. Right, let me show you how to get
uphill and then we'll do the whole thing over
again.'

Laughter was the first thing Finn heard as he
walked around the side of the house. Loud
peals of pure and unadulterated laughter.
His chest tightened and he stopped to listen.
When was the last time he had heard Saffy
laugh like that? Like the child she was rather
than a solemn miniature adult, weighed down
by responsibilities and cares he couldn't persuade her to relinquish. Yet here she was, giggling away.

He walked forward, the snow crunching
under his feet, taking a moment to take the

day in. The air was still crisp but the sky was an impossible blue, the snow millions of bright crystals under the sun's spotlight.

After a couple of days of typical British travel chaos, with gridlocked roads, cancelled trains and supermarkets running out of bread, the country had returned to sheepish normality. With the temperature cold enough to preserve the snow, but the weather fine enough for the roads to be cleared, Blakeley had enjoyed a steady influx of visitors, coming to enjoy the wintry hiking trails or, for the younger visitors, to meet Father Christmas in his real-life sleigh. Visitors of all ages finished their visit with hot chocolate, coffee or mulled wine and delicious homemade treats in the café.

The school holidays had started today, and as a result Blakeley was buzzing. Not that it was apparent here, where there were no signposts or trails to lure visitors.

'Saffy?'

He reached the top of the terrace and looked over the sloping hill leading to the fields of the tenant farm, now snow-covered and bare apart from a scattering of sheep in the distance. To his amazement he saw his eldest niece gliding to the bottom of the hill on a pair of skis, slowly, but with a confidence he hadn't seen before. Alongside her was Alex, her usually pale cheeks pink, whether with cold or excitement he couldn't tell, her eyes sparkling.

'Hi, there,' he called, and both females stopped and turned. Saffy promptly fell over, clutching at Alex as she did so, who tumbled on top of her. Finn held his breath, relieved when they both started laughing again.

'Don't try and join us, Finn,' Alex warned when she'd sobered up a little and helped Saffy get back to her feet. 'The snow has frozen on top and it's really icy. We'll head back to you.'

'Been having fun?' he enquired, and Saffy lifted a glowing face to smile at him.

'Skiing is the best!'

'Is that so?' He grinned as he looked at the tracks in the snow. 'Did you know that I learnt to ski right here too?' With the exact same teacher.

He risked a glance at Alex, all kitted out against the snow, and his whole body heated at the way her hair was slipping out of her hat and at the natural colour in her cheeks. She looked utterly wholesome and absolutely adorable, and Finn couldn't quite remember just why they had decided not to repeat Monday afternoon's activities.

No. He could. And they were all very worthy and sensible reasons. But the main one was that he knew that it was too dangerous. He'd been in love with her once. He so easily could be again. Maybe he was. Maybe he had always been.

But one afternoon didn't cure a lifetime of hurt. He wasn't naïve enough to believe that—although Alex did seem a lot less brittle, more optimistic. But her future wasn't here, where she would be trapped by her past. And his was. The girls were happy here, and he had promised them stability. If he jeopardised that then he would be no better than Nicky.

'Go on, then,' he said to Saffy as she reached him. 'Show me how it's done. Thank you,' he added to Alex. 'This is really kind of you.'

'There's no need to thank me!'

She smiled at him and Finn's heart turned over. Was she feeling it too? This yearning? This sense of belonging?

'I enjoyed it. She's a really lovely girl. You should be so proud of her.'

'I am. Of them both.'

They didn't speak while Saffy set off, then Finn yelled encouragement as his niece sailed to the bottom of the slope. He applauded her enthusiastically and she gave him a shy wave before starting her journey back to the top of the hill.

'She's doing really well. But of course you are an amazing skier yourself. I'm surprised this slope isn't driving you mad with boredom.'

'I haven't skied in years. To be honest I didn't come here for the sport but for work. I had this idea of doing some really short videos of myself, all in Hawk ski gear, out and about enjoying the estate. From my perspective, so it could be anyone. It would be a double reinforcing of the clothes being used in the snow and also all the Christmas things we have on offer.'

The 'we' warmed him through.

She's just doing her job, he reminded himself.

'That's a great idea.'

'I want to do some filming around the castle too, now it's really open and being visited.'

'The place is buzzing. Loads of people are enjoying the Christmas Through the Ages exhibition in the castle and even more are out and about. I've checked that the treetop trails aren't accessible. With this ice it would be a health and safety nightmare if some kid got up there and slipped. But everything else is very much open for business.'

'It's amazing to see the estate so alive. It used to be so exclusive, and in a way I loved the privacy and secrecy of it. But this is good too.'

'It seemed so sad when I first came home. The village neglected and more and more people leaving. The castle all closed up; the gardens barely maintained. It seemed at times like I'd never hack my way through everything that needed doing to get it open for this Christmas. People advised me to wait until the New Year but I knew it could be done.'

'Why was opening for Christmas so important?'

Finn glanced at Saffy as she padded towards them, panting and beaming, and lowered his voice. 'To tackle the elephant in the room straight on. To show that I know what happened here at Christmas ten years ago and move the conversation on. I didn't want a whole year of the anniversary looming on the horizon.'

Alex didn't betray her intimacy with the elephant by even a flicker of her eyes. 'Very sensible. I probably would have advised doing the same. And it's worked. I've been out and about all week and most people are talking about the amazing Tudor marchpane house or the Edwardian tree, not the Beaumonts. Congratulations, Finn.'

She looked over at Saffy.

'That's brilliant, Saffy. You are doing so well. If I were you, I would try and persuade your uncle to take you skiing. I think a few proper lessons and you'd be away.'

'Can I, Uncle Finn?' Saffy's pleading eyes were huge in her thin face. 'That would be the coolest thing ever.'

Finn reached out and tousled his niece's hair. 'Sure.'

'When? This winter? Can I go these holidays? Christmas isn't for five days. We could go now.'

'And miss the play rehearsals?'

Saffy shrugged. 'We already did the play once. Oh, Uncle Finn, please can I go skiing soon?'

'We'll see.' The quintessential adult response.

Her face fell and he cursed inwardly. Oh, to be nine and think that the world was that simple. That you could just decide to go skiing and go. It had been like that for him once, post-university and pre-Hawk, when he had worked his way around the world, deciding direction and timetable on a whim. In those days he'd been as likely to head to the mountains and ski as to the sea to surf. Not the stable life he had promised his nieces, but fun.

Their life with Nicky had been full of their mother's impulse decisions. Finn had vowed to give them the safety of itineraries and timetables and annual planners. Their schoolwork and activities were plotted out on the blackboard in the kitchen. Every appointment was programmed into his phone. He knew clothes sizes and shoe sizes and the name of the woman who cut their hair. They were safe.

But as his gaze snagged Alex's he knew that wasn't enough. He couldn't keep the girls wrapped up in bubble wrap, much as he wanted to. Alex had wrapped herself up and hidden herself away for all her adult life, and maybe she'd been safe, but her life was only half lived. Never sad, maybe, but never truly happy. His greatest gift would be to teach the girls happiness.

'I have to make a quick work call,' he said. 'Keep going, Saffy. I'll time you when I get back.'

'Can Alex film me? And put it online? I'm all in Hawk clothes.'

Finn had a strict no publicity rule for the girls. He had seen what constant exposure had done to Alex, and that had been in a pre-social media age.

He looked at Alex and she shrugged. 'I could make sure her face wasn't in it. Just the back of her head. But it's your call.'

'Let me see it and then I'll decide. Fair, Saffy?'

'I guess… I need to see it too, Alex. I don't want me falling over online, even if you can't see my face.'

'Understood.'

Finn watched for a moment as Saffy set off with a stylish flourish, Alex filming her. Anyone looking at them would assume they were a family. The situation felt so domestic, so right. With a sigh, half for what might have been and half for what was to come, he headed back around the corner to make his call.

Less than five minutes later he was back, to find Saffy and Alex squinting over Alex's phone. They looked up as he hailed them, and Finn was unable to keep the smug smile off his face.

'Okay, Saffy,' he said. 'I've managed to get us a ski lodge for two nights and lessons for you and Scarlett this afternoon and tomorrow morning. Kaitlin is booking us flights right now. So, you need to go and pack for yourself and Scarlett. Warm clothes. I'll get you ski trousers, a jacket, gloves and a hat, but you need clothes for underneath, PJs, and dresses or jeans for the evening. I'll come and check in an hour. Toothbrushes, too. Scarlett's over at Polly's so we'll grab her on the way to the airport. What?'

Both Alex and Saffy were staring at him, with identical expressions of surprise on their faces.

'I thought you wanted to go skiing?' he said.

'I... I do. We're really going? Today?' Saffy's face was so full of hope it hurt him to look at her.

'If we're ready and don't miss the flight, yes. You'll only get a couple of hours this afternoon, but all day tomorrow and Monday morning. Oh, and don't forget your cossies—the hotel has a hot tub.'

Saffy threw her arms around him, almost overbalancing on her skis as she did so. 'Thank you, Uncle Finn. Thank you.'

'You deserve it,' he said gruffly. 'You had to change schools yet again when we moved here, and you've done really well. And don't think I don't see you looking out for your little sister. Father Christmas thought you deserved an extra early present and I agreed.'

'Father Christmas?'

'Who do you think I was just talking to? Go on, Saffy, get those skis off and start packing.'

'If you leave the skis and boots here I'll put them away,' Alex said. She smiled at the girl. 'I can't wait to hear all about it.'

'Why don't you come too?' Saffy said. 'Can she, Uncle Finn? Alex hasn't been skiing for ages, and she's really good.'

'Oh, I don't…'

'I'm not sure she'd…'

They both spoke at once, and Finn gestured for Alex to go first.

'It's a family trip, Saffy, but thank you for thinking of me. Besides, I have my work here. I was planning on filming, remember? It will be good to have lots of footage for the next few days.'

'Scarlett and I won't mind you being there,' Saffy reassured her. 'Nor would Uncle Finn.' She looked up at Finn imploringly.

His first instinct was to agree with Alex. She did have work to do, and it was a family trip. But the words wouldn't come. She hadn't skied for years…why not invite her along?

Because you're supposed to be maintaining some boundaries, especially around the girls.

He looked over at Alex and knew that, although she was hiding it really well, possibly even from herself, she wanted to come.

'There's plenty of room for one more. And you could get lots of great footage of Hawk ski-wear. We'll be back Monday afternoon, so you can film here then.'

'I have been meaning to talk to you about featuring you much more prominently online. After all, the brand is all you. You named it after yourself. It's based on your lifestyle. Footage of you out on the slopes would be a great start. But...'

'No buts. That's settled. I'll let Kaitlin know, email her your passport details. Help yourself to anything you need from the stockroom. I'll see you out front in an hour.'

She stood there, bottom lip caught between her teeth as she considered, evidently torn.

'Please, Alex,' Saffy begged from the bench where she was wrestling with her skis.

Alex nodded, more to herself than them. 'Okay.'

'Okay?'

'Yes. Yes, I'll come. Thank you, Finn. Saffy, hand me those skis. Pack warm things. I'll see you soon.'

With a swish of her ponytail she was gone, handling both pairs of skis and boots effortlessly. A small hand stole into Finn's and he looked down at Saffy.

'I like Alex,' she said, with a little wistful sigh that tore at Finn's heart. 'I wish she wasn't leaving at Christmas.

'Me too, kiddo. Me too.' He ruffled her hair again. 'Come on, let's get going.'

And as Saffy skipped towards the house, her movements graceful on the firm snow, Finn knew that by inviting Alex along this weekend he was making her inevitable departure harder for everyone. But he wanted to give her something to remember. He wanted to remind her just what fun life could be. That was his gift to her.

He just hoped the personal cost wouldn't be too high.

CHAPTER ELEVEN

'THAT WAS THE best day ever!' Scarlett couldn't stop yawning as she spoke and Saffy joined in. Both girls' heads were drooping onto the table.

Alex laughed. 'I have never seen two such tired girls. You've not even finished your chocolate cake.'

'Bed for you two as soon as you finish your dinner.' Finn reached out and snagged a piece of cake off Scarlett's plate. She only half-heartedly swatted him away.

'I'm not tired.' She yawned again.

'I am,' Alex said frankly. 'A whole day of skiing when you're not used to it would exhaust anyone. And isn't Anton meeting you two bright and early for your last lesson? You want to be well rested so you can show him how much you've learnt.'

'Yes!' Scarlett brightened.

Both girls had taken immediately to their

handsome and engaging young instructor, who was clearly used to children and beginners. After an anxious first hour Finn had relaxed enough to allow Alex to coax him up to the slopes, secure in the knowledge that the girls were in experienced hands.

'Maybe I *will* go to bed, Uncle Finn.'

'Right…'

Finn looked so discombobulated it was hard for Alex not to laugh.

'If I'd known you were going to say those words I'd have had my phone ready to record them, as proof that Scarlett Hawkin chose to go to bed of her own volition. You heard her.'

'You are silly.' But Scarlett didn't demur when Finn lifted her from her seat. 'G'night, Alex.'

'Night, Scarlett. Sweet dreams.'

'I'm off too,' Saffron said, sliding off her chair. 'Night.'

To Alex's surprise Saffron gave her a small, clumsy hug before joining her uncle and sister. From the look on Finn's face, he was as surprised by the girl's display of spontaneous affection as Alex had been—and as moved.

As Finn shepherded the girls out of the room Alex managed to get to her feet, muscles pressed into action all day after being unused for too long protesting at the movement, and gathered the girls' plates to carry through to the small galley kitchen. A kitchen that was mostly for show, as the cluster of lodges situated by a icy lake were supplied with all meals by the hotel to which they belonged.

Small but comfortably designed, the lodges had a heated outer room, for skis, jackets and other winter clothing to dry overnight, and one huge sitting and dining room, with windows at the back looking out over the lake. The floor was heated, but a huge oil burning stove still dominated the room, chucking out impressive amounts of heat. A staircase at the side led up to two bedrooms, both with their own bathrooms, and a further bedroom, where the girls slept, was tucked into the attic. The décor was very minimalist and tasteful, all greys and creams, with splashes of colour, but comfortable and cosy as opposed to stark and modern, and enhanced by the silver and cream Christmas tree in the corner and other seasonal decorations.

After rinsing and stacking the plates, Alex collected her barely touched wine and moved over to the vast sofa, tucking herself into the corner from where she could see the lit-up lake and some intrepid ice skaters in the distance. She listened to the almost inaudible giggles and talk from above as Finn chivvied the girls into bed. Any minute now he'd be down, and then they would have the whole evening together. Alex's stomach clenched at the thought of the torturous intimacy. Of looking but not touching.

Last night hadn't been too bad. After managing three hours on the slopes they'd all headed to the hotel to use the pool and the hot tubs, and had eaten there with a contact of Finn's who owned the resort—and stocked Hawk clothing in his hotel boutique. They'd stayed on to watch the entertainment, and by the time they'd got back to the lodge they'd all been ready to head straight to bed, knowing they had an early start.

But even with the exercise, fresh air, good food and wine it had still taken Alex far too long to get to sleep, knowing that Finn was just over the corridor. All the reasons for staying in her room were as valid as they had been back at Blakeley: the girls, her own imminent departure, the knowledge that the more time she spent with him the harder moving on would be. But his proximity had made those excellent reasons seem less and less persuadable.

Today was no better. All evening she had been hyper-aware of his proximity, of his every word, every movement, her body reacting to each accidental touch. She wanted him. That afternoon in the cottage in the woods hadn't slaked her desire, it had heightened it.

Maybe she should plead tiredness and head up herself, or go out for a walk…

'I've been thinking.'

Alex jumped as Finn spoke. She hadn't heard him come back downstairs, so lost in her thoughts.

'Why don't we go out for dinner? The hotel offers a babysitting service.'

'It might be too late to get someone,' she said, but the thought appealed. Out. Where there were lots of other people. No intimacy, but crowds. 'But it would be nice to see something of the village while we're here. Gorgeous as the hotel is, I'd like to explore a little further.'

'In that case I'll see what I can do.'

Alex took a sip of her wine and gazed out at the lake while she waited for Finn to return. If he couldn't get a babysitter then she needed a plan: she'd order something quick and light off the extensive menu, talk about work until it arrived and then go straight to bed. No more wine, no lingering glances, and no personal chat. It would be fine. She could absolutely do this. Even if she didn't want to.

'All sorted.' Finn stood opposite her, phone

still in his hand. 'I'll just go and tell the girls; I'd hate for them to be alarmed if they wake.'

'Great. I'd better put on some lipstick if we're heading out. Maybe a dress.'

She looked down at her jeans and jumper, both from the Hawk range and both chosen for comfort rather than high fashion. Her friends would barely recognise her. She had a reputation for being exquisitely and tastefully dressed, no matter what her budget. But being with Finn and the girls made her feel comfortable, as if she didn't need her usual armour.

When she re-joined Finn downstairs, twenty minutes later, her armour was firmly in place. She'd picked a long-sleeved red flowery midi-dress, nipped in at the waist, teamed with wool tights—it was cold out, after all—boots and a chunky gold necklace. After some deliberation she'd let her hair stay loose, merely brushing it and tucking it behind her ears.

'You look lovely,' Finn said as she picked up her coat.

His tone was mild, but when she turned to smile her thanks the look in his eyes made her shiver.

'So do you. Nice to see you in a suit, not a fleece.'

'When we start a tailored menswear division I'll wear more suits.'

'I'll look forward to it.'

Before he could answer there was a soft knock at the door and Finn opened it, ushering in a capable-looking young woman who, in a strong Australian accent, introduced herself as Michelle, one of the seasonal workers who enjoyed bed, board and ski passes in return for bar work, waitressing shifts and other duties, such as babysitting.

Alex gave Finn five minutes to question Michelle on everything from first aid to fire safety, her stomach twisting all the time. She had thought going out would be the better of two evils, but they both looked so smart it felt more like a date.

Well, why couldn't it be? In just two days it would be Christmas Eve. She'd go home and this time they'd part as friends. But part they would. Why not enjoy one date first, as if they were living that alternate might-have-been life?

The Alex who had first set foot in Blakeley would be horrified by the idea. But that Alex wouldn't be here, in a ski resort in the Austrian Alps, in the first place. She'd been left behind in that cottage in the woods, and her newer, braver incarnation was taking her first cautious steps into the future. Why not start with an evening to remember?

'Come on, Finn.' She slipped an arm through his and smiled at Michelle. 'You have both our numbers? We won't be far. And do order anything you want. There's tea and coffee in the kitchen, and obviously there's room service for food or soft drinks.'

It was cold out, but fresh, and Alex was glad of her Hawk down coat, even if it wasn't as stylish as the long wool coat she wore in London. Her feet were snug inside her lined boots, her hands protected by gloves.

Although snow lay all around, thick and deep, the paths had been either cleared or gritted, making walking easy throughout the hotel grounds and into the small Alpine village. It had been dark for several hours and streetlights lit the pretty chalet-lined streets. Lights beamed out of hotels, cafés, shops and bars, where the après-ski hour was well and truly going strong, ensuring the town buzzed with activity. Christmas lights were strung across the streets, adding a festive air to the surroundings, and as they neared the village square Alex saw a huge Christmas tree, glaring with red, gold and cream lights and baubles.

As they had left the house Finn had taken

her hand in his, and after a startled moment she had let him. They were both in thick gloves, no skin to skin at all, yet she fancied she could sense his pulse beating in time with hers.

'So, what do you want to do first? A drink? Or go straight to eat?'

'I don't mind. It's not often I have time to just wander. It's quite nice.'

Finn squeezed her hand. 'Then let's wander.'

They walked slowly through the packed centre of the village, browsing the enticing shop windows and eventually stopping in front of a shop selling traditional dirndls.

'I can just imagine my friends' faces if they opened parcels with those inside on Christmas Day,' Alex said as she took in the intricate embroidery and lace. 'They'd think I'd gone mad. But they're so pretty. I'd love to have an excuse to buy one. Would the girls like them?'

Finn shrugged. 'Where clothes are concerned I have no clue. A T-shirt can be the favourite thing one moment and the most despised the next. I defy the most accomplished data scientist to forecast Scarlett's sartorial choices.'

'I'll still have a look, if that's okay with you? I'd like to get them something and I've been so busy I haven't had a chance.'

The shop was filled with traditional costumes and accessories of all colours and types, and after some thought Alex bought traditional filigree silver heart necklaces for the girls. Scarlett's on a red ribbon and Saffron's on bright yellow.

'I never thought I'd be so clichéd as to match ribbon colours to names,' Alex said as she paid. 'But they can always change them if they hate them. Are you sure you don't want some lederhosen? I'm happy to get them for you?'

'That's very kind, but a gentleman always buys his own lederhosen.'

Tucking the two necklaces into her bag, Alex followed Finn out of the shop, freezing as she looked into the window of the next shop along. The window dazzled, showcasing glass and crystal, wine glasses and vases—and hundreds of Christmas tree ornaments.

She glanced at Finn to find him looking at her, his expression one of nostalgia and regret. 'Do you want to go in?' he asked.

'I haven't bought a Christmas tree ornament since I left Blakeley,' she said, unable to maintain eye contact, fixing her gaze on the sparkling display instead. 'I love it that you did, though. You wouldn't let me buy you lederhosen, but maybe I can buy you an ornament instead. How about that one?' She pointed to a little mouse holding a pair of skis.

'Yes, the girls will like that one. But I have one condition.'

'A condition?' She still couldn't look at him, feeling unaccountably shy.

'That I choose one for you. But you can't open it until Christmas day.'

That didn't sound like too much of a condition. Amber was bound to have put up a Christmas tree in the office. It would be nice to have something of her own to put on it. 'Okay.'

She turned to walk into the shop and Finn put a hand on her arm.

'And one more condition.'

She looked up at him then, and her breath caught at the tenderness and desire in his eyes.

'That you let me thank you properly.'

His kiss was light but, oh, so sweet, and after a moment's surprise Alex kissed him back, uttering a small cry of protest when he drew away, her fingers still entangled in his hair.

'I thought we'd agreed not to?' Her voice shook slightly. She still held on to him, unable to quite let go, and Finn smiled down at her.

'We did. But maybe we were too hasty in

our decision-making. After all, here we are in this beautiful place, enjoying each other's company. I'm happy to bend the rules a little if you are.'

Was she? Should she? The sensible answer was no, of course not. But she'd bypassed sense when it came to Finn Hawkin a long time ago.

'I'm all in favour of a little rule-bending now and then.'

His smile widened. 'In that case, let me thank you again. I don't think I got it quite right last time.'

The village was full of restaurants and cafés to fit every inclination and budget. Finn found them a table at a small intimate restaurant overlooking the lake, where the atmosphere wasn't too loud or glitzy and there were no groups of weekenders enjoying shots at the bar, nor tables of bankers ordering bottles of champagne as they lived out their rock star dreams.

The food was simple but good, everything was cooked perfectly, and the décor was a little traditional but not too touristy. It was perfect.

Alex was perfect too. Dangerously so. She was relaxed, seemingly happy. She had no edge tonight, no wariness. She asked and answered questions, chatted inconsequentially about frivolous things like TV programmes they both enjoyed, music and books.

She listened, too, as Finn opened up about how complicated his feelings were about taking his nieces to live with him, about the feeling of guilt that he had deprived his sister of her children and the girls of their mother, the worry that he had acted too soon, the even bigger regret that he hadn't acted sooner. He touched on his father's death, and shared some of the stories from the first year of Hawk, when money had been so tight he'd lived in a student house, only for the brand to soar when a celebrity snowboarder had been photographed in one of their jackets.

'It's been a surreal journey,' he said at last. 'Hard work, but worth it.'

'It's been really interesting today. I filmed you a little, but I was also doing vox pops with some skiers and snowboarders who were in Hawk ski-wear. They all feel a real connection to the brand and to your values. They're making a definite statement when they buy your clothes. It's inspiring, and there's a lot you can do with that. I know Penelope already works with some influencers and successful surfers and climbers, but I'd suggest aligning yourself with people who share your values too. Eco-warriors and environmentalists…people who want to make a difference, to change the world. Have you found someone to cover the rest of Penelope's time off?'

'Not yet. I don't suppose you would stay on?'

He was only half joking and her smile was full of regret.

'I don't think that would be a good idea. Things are already complicated. Besides, I'm needed back in Chelsea. With Harriet's wedding this year, and Emilia's engagement surely on the horizon, there will be a lot to do. And over the last two weeks I've looked at what you've achieved, and I have to say I am a little envious. My goals were smaller, safer. I knew I wanted to work in PR, but I hadn't thought too far beyond being good at my job and where that might take me.'

'You *are* good at your job,' he interjected, and she smiled at him.

'Thank you. It's always good to have happy clients. I wanted to be head of and own my own agency. To have control, to be safe. And the last few months have been more successful than we could have imagined. Emilia is working on huge international events. I was in New York just before I came to you, working with a lifestyle brand who want to expand into the UK. Harriet's been placing PAs all over the world, and the demand for British trained nannies is so huge Amber is seriously considering setting up a section to focus on that area. We could be properly international. A household name.'

'You could.' It was brilliant to see her like this, inspired by the future, lit up with ambition, just as she had used to be. 'What do your partners think?'

'I haven't discussed it with them yet. To be honest, Finn, I don't think they'll be so actively involved in the future. Deangelo travels so much and Harriet likes to go with him. When Laurent proposes, Emilia's life will change completely. And as for Amber... Amber definitely wants marriage and a family of her own. It's just a matter of time.'

Finn desperately wanted to ask about *her* plans beyond work. Did she want marriage too? A family? But he knew what the answer would be. Why would a girl whose life had been destroyed by her family, who had never known unconditional love, aspire to love and marriage? If he'd been free, then maybe he could have tried to help her. To give her the time and love she didn't know she needed.

But he wasn't free.

How he wished he was.

'Tell me about them…your friends.'

He should have been there to help her when everyone had failed her. He couldn't help but be curious about the women who had stepped in where he had faltered. The women Alex clearly thought of as her family.

Alex took a sip of her wine. 'What do you want to know?'

'When did you meet?'

'One Christmas Eve. Not a good day for me, as you know. We all worked together, for Deangelo Santos, but we didn't know each other well—it's a huge company. I was head of PR, Harriet was Deangelo's PA, Emilia managed events and Amber was in charge of looking after visiting clients and their families. We might have been in the same meetings, but we didn't know each other. But on Christmas Eve four years ago we all had reasons not to leave early and bumped into each other on the way out of the office. It was clear none of us had anywhere to be, so we spent the evening together—and met up the next day for a walk. It was the best Christmas I'd had for a long time.'

'Why were the others alone?'

It almost physically hurt Finn to hear her loneliness laid out so starkly. He looked over at her, soft and warm in the candlelight, but with that glittering edge she'd always had, and knew with a shattering certainty that now Alex was back in his life he would never allow her to be lonely again.

He'd thought he was too busy to fall in love before. Too invested in his work, choosing Hawk before relationships time and time again, and only faintly regretful when that choice led to break-ups. But maybe he had never fallen out of love with Alex, the determined girl he'd grown up alongside. The only person he had ever really counted on. No wonder it had wounded him so badly when she'd turned on him.

Their reasons for parting this Christmas Eve were valid. Alex wanted to return to London, and his life was at Blakeley. He'd promised himself no relationships. Not while the girls lived with him, and not unless he was pretty damn sure the relationship would be a for ever one—and who could make that guarantee? But he had known and loved Alex his whole life. There had to be a way to make them work if she wanted to as well. And he was as sure as he could be that she did. He just didn't think she knew it yet.

Alex poured them both some water and sat back. 'Harriet's dad has dementia. She'd been

looking after him since school and was really
isolated. Emilia didn't get on with her dad and
stepfamily, and Amber was estranged from
hers. I don't know the details; we don't pry
and we don't have to tell. There's an unspoken
pact, I guess, not to ask. We've spent the last
three Christmases together. It will be weird
this year without Harriet and Emilia…' Her
voice trailed off.

'Stay with us,' Finn offered. 'Your friend
is very welcome too. The girls would love it.'

It was a spontaneous response, but the more
he thought about it, the more sense it made.

'We're having a small Christmas too.
There's plenty of space. Show your friend
where you were brought up.'

'She doesn't know. About before. None of
them do. Only you.' She stared down at her
empty plate. 'They're the people I am closest
to in the world and they know nothing about
me. I let no one in, Finn.'

'You've let me in. I'm here. I'm not going
anywhere. Whenever you want me you just
have to ask. No, don't even ask. Tell me.'

'Finn…'

He laid his hand over hers, their fingers
slotting together as if they were made to fit.
'I mean it, Alex. We've wasted so much time
through misunderstandings and fear and hurt.'

He took a deep breath, trying to figure out the next step, not wanting to scare her off, but needing her to know exactly how he felt. That this time he was in—all in.

But at that moment the glamorous woman at the table next to them, whom Finn had noticed eying him several times over the last hour, leaned over and tapped his arm.

'Finn Hawkin? Is that you? How lovely to see you.'

Damn. Finn smiled automatically, his brain trying to compute who the woman might be. As he did so he noticed Alex stiffen and shrink back in her seat.

'It's been too long, but you are looking amazing,' he said.

It must have been the right response because the woman beamed. 'The Hawk campaign feels like a lifetime ago.'

He was on solid ground here. 'You look younger than ever.'

'I wish! Five years is a long time, especially in this game.'

'Not at all,' he said. 'We're just lucky to have people like you representing Hawk. Are you enjoying the season?' He turned to the mystery model's companion, hoping for some clues, and was rewarded when she beamed at him.

'Antoinette. Lady Antoinette Anstruther. I was at school with Spiffy here.'

Right. Spiffy.

That narrowed it down. It was like one of those hideous parties Alex used to have, when every girl he met had been called Flopsy or Bunny or Popsy, as if they were characters in a children's book. He'd never understood the upper class penchant for saddling children with a string of long and unpronounceable names and then shortening them to something infantile.

He thought hard and recognition finally dawned. 'So how are you, Sofia? Are you still modelling?'

'Oh, no. I gave it all up when I got engaged to Jimsy. In fact, that's why I'm here—joint hen and stag dos skiing over Christmas. Toni and I are the advance party. I can't believe I ran into you. Everyone is talking about how you bought Blakeley. No one believes me when I tell them that I met you there before, with Lolz.' Her laugh was as high as it was false. 'It's amazing to think I knew you back then. You always did have that brooding Mellors thing going on, even as a teenager. We all had quite the crush, but Lola made it very clear we could look but not touch.'

Alex had become so self-effacing during

the conversation she might have turned invisible, and neither woman gave her as much as a glance. Finn couldn't look at her as he replied. 'That was a long time ago.'

'Not that long...'

Sofia stopped speaking, waiting as the waiter came over to remove their plates, and as Alex murmured a quick thank-you her attention shifted. Finn could see the moment recognition hit her, blue eyes widening and mouth opening.

'Lolz? Is it you? Oh, my God, Lola Beaumont. Where have you been?'

CHAPTER TWELVE

'THE SITUATION IS completely manageable.' Finn strode down the path, mouth set.

Alex understood his reaction, even though she didn't agree. He assumed that every situation could be controlled. After all, he was used to calling the shots. Thought a simple 'no comment' would suffice. But he must know this wasn't going to happen this time.

He'd been there when the story broke last time. Had driven through the crowds of photographers, seen the headlines. Did he really think that the sighting of a missing It Girl and the realisation that she'd been working back at her scandalous old home wouldn't create a media storm? That the whole saga wouldn't be raked over again and again? That those photos wouldn't find their way back onto front pages?

Her stomach tightened, nausea writhing around inside her.

It was all going to happen again.

Maybe exposure had been inevitable from the moment she'd found herself at Blakeley. Or from the minute Emilia had been catapulted into the public eye. She should have known that she couldn't hide for ever. But to be discovered at Blakeley on the anniversary of the tragedy was nothing short of a disaster. She was a mistress of spin, but she had no idea how to handle this.

She looked at her hands and realised they were shaking, but she couldn't feel them. She didn't even feel sick any more. She was numb.

'Plausible deniability.'

It was amazing, under the circumstances, how she could sound so calm. As if her carefully put-together life *wasn't* about to be blown into smithereens.

'If Sofia goes to the press, or her friend does, you go with plausible deniability. You employed Alexandra Davenport to work on the reopening of Blakeley Castle. You haven't seen Lola Beaumont in years, and you have no idea if Lola and your temporary employee are the same person, but you doubt it. Meanwhile I'll prepare a statement saying that we provided you with PR support and have no prior acquaintance. Hopefully no one will dig any deeper. Even better, maybe Sofia will forget about seeing me. Either way, we need a plan, and I think it's definitely for the best if I head straight back to London tonight. I can handle the rest of the work from there. You don't actually need me on site. We'll monitor the situation. At least we didn't confirm anything to Sofia. She might just decide she was wrong.'

But she knew that hope was futile. Even when Finn had introduced Alex and explained that she was just a colleague she'd seen the disbelief in her old friend's eyes. The chances of her not telling anyone about her suspicions were slim to none.

Sofia might not go to the press herself, but she wouldn't be able to help gossiping. And, maybe not today, maybe not tomorrow, but at some point a journalist was going to start looking into the co-founder of the Happy Ever After Agency. The links to her godmother and the address in Chelsea were there for anyone who knew what they were looking for.

'So what if they do dig?'

Alex blinked. Surely she must have misunderstood. 'Sorry?'

'So what if they realise who you are? What difference does it make?'

What difference did it make? How could he even ask that?

'I thought you wanted your nieces kept safe? Any suggestion that Lola Beaumont has been back at Blakeley and they can wave goodbye to a normal life for weeks. There will be cameras at every gate, journalists at every event. Your life, Nicky's, your father's will be exhumed and picked over. Our prior acquaintance—everything. You escaped the scrutiny last time, Finn. Believe me, you don't want to be the target this time.'

'It will be uncomfortable for a few days, but it will die down. Alex, the girls love you. *I* love you. I always have. If the truth is out there, then what does it matter? You could make your home at Blakeley. Figure out who you are and what you want with us by your side. No one will bother you; you'll be safe.' He stopped and turned her to face him, dark eyes burning. 'I love you, Alex.'

Alex couldn't meet his intense gaze. His words echoed around and around her head, and her hands were shaking harder. She clasped them together, trying to still them. He'd said he loved her. Finn Hawkin, her one constant, the boy who had made her childhood happy, the man who had saved her, woken her from a decade's half-life, loved her.

For one moment she felt his heat coursing through her, warming her, and the tantalising possibility of a future with him flashed through her mind like the end credits of a movie. All she had to do was say the words trembling on her lips, words she had said only to him, and that future could be hers. A life of laughter and companionship and love. A life in which she would fall asleep and wake up next to this man. A life back home at Blakeley. A life with two girls who needed to be shown that happiness was possible.

The words withered and died. How could she, of all people, give them stability? How could she trust that what they shared now would last? How could she even trust in this? Finn said he loved her, but she was a lie. She always had been.

'I can't.'

'Why not?'

She couldn't look at him. Instead she started walking again, almost at a trot. The hotel gates were within view, and that meant the lodge was less than five minutes away. She could be packed and out through the door within an hour. On the first plane back to London by dawn. Home by morning. The thought of the Chelsea townhouse, her own bedroom, safety, was almost overwhelming.

'I've enjoyed this walk down memory lane, Finn, but that's all it was.'

'Nonsense. Don't lie to me, Alex. I know you. What happened earlier this week, this evening, wasn't just nostalgia.'

'You love Lola, Finn. You want me to be her. Well, I'm not. She's gone and she won't be coming back. I'm sorry but you have to move on. I have.'

There was a long silence before he spoke, and when he did his voice was hoarse with emotion—with passion, with sincerity and with sorrow. Sorrow she had caused. The pain of it ripped through her.

'The boy I was loved Lola, yes. But even then I knew that Lola wore a mask, even with me. And when I met you again you wore a mask too, but I saw through it. I see through it now. You know what I think? I think the real you is somewhere in between. Not as reckless as Lola, not as guarded as Alex. I think the real you sent those photos to me that night and that's why you were so very hurt when they were leaked. Lola would have turned their existence into a PR campaign. I think it was the real you a week ago, in the cottage, and it's the real you tonight. I think that the real you loves my girls and understands them, and they love her. I think I have a chance at a really happy future with you. But I get that you're scared. I get that letting people in is hard. But trust me, Alex. Trust in love.'

'This summer I told Emilia the same thing. I told her to trust in love, and she did. But she's different to me.' She had difficulty speaking, her voice so small she wasn't sure he'd even heard her.

'How?'

She winced at the catch in his voice.

'Why is she different?'

'It's not just us, Finn. It's my past and your girls and Blakeley itself. I can't be there. I just can't. Even if Sofia miraculously tells nobody someone will recognise me eventually, in the local shop or in the village. I can't hide in the cottage and the office for ever. And I can't be recognised.'

'Alex, you did nothing wrong. Your parents' sins are not yours.'

'But I ended up paying. Finn, I've worked so hard to protect myself. Please don't ask me to undo all that work. Please don't ask me to be vulnerable. Please don't ask to be let in.'

'I don't want to ask. I want you to welcome me in. You don't have to do this alone, Alex.'

If only she could believe him. 'I do. I have always had to. It's the only way I'm safe. Don't you see that, Finn?'

'So tonight, last week, all we've shared, all

we've been, all we are, means nothing? You are just going to walk away?'

'We could be friends,' she suggested, aware of what a poor offer 'friends' was compared to the love he had so openly offered. 'You and I could see each other sometimes…if we were careful.'

It wasn't much, but it was all she had.

It was Finn's turn to shake his head, his eyes darker than ever with sorrow. 'I've said all along that I can't embark on any relationship that puts the girls' security at risk. Sneaking around to see you sometimes isn't something that works for them or me. We deserve more.'

Alex swallowed. 'It's all or nothing? Is that it?'

'I never said any differently,' Finn said gently.

He stopped again, tugging gently at her hand to get her to stop too. Reluctantly she stilled, allowed him to turn her to face him, allowed his hand to tilt her chin so she met his eyes.

'What we have, Alex, it's pretty special. Not many people get to be with someone who knows them so completely. Not everyone gets to right the past. We can do both. Sure, it's scary. I get that. I'm scared too. There's so much at stake. But I believe in us. I believe in you. I always did. Believe in me, Alex.'

How she wanted to. How she wanted to lean against his broad shoulder and allow Finn to carry her through life.

He hadn't sold those photos, had never betrayed her. He hadn't destroyed them. She had. She was as reckless with people's lives and hearts as her parents. How could a person who had never known stability and unconditional love offer it? She wouldn't just be screwing up her life or Finn's life if she got it wrong, there were Scarlett and Saffron to consider. She recognised a kindred spirit in Saffron, seeing a girl scared that she wasn't good enough, ready for rejection. What if she messed her up even more?

'Damn you, Finn,' she whispered, and his grip tightened.

'Believe in me,' he said again.

She reached to cover his hand with hers. 'I do. I always did. But I don't believe in *me*. I don't know how to and I need to figure that out. Being back with you, loving you, has shown me the way. Shown me that maybe I can reach for more than security, that I can have ambitions and hope. Thank you for that. But I'm not safe, Finn. Not just because I could find myself back on the front pages at any time, or because my very presence could disrupt your home and your business, but because I don't know how to be part of a family. I can't take the risk that one day you'll realise I'm not enough. I don't trust myself to be what the girls need...'

'Alex, we all feel like that. I feel like that every day. There's no rule book—not for parenting or for love. All we can do is our best. That's the secret.'

'Finn. When I'm with you I feel anchored. I always did. But it's just another act. Nothing about me is real—not even my name. My whole life is about spin, from my job to the way I want people to see me. I want you to love me. I always did. But how do you know I'm not spinning you? Being the person you want me to be? How do I know that?'

'Because I have always known you, and I have always seen you. Doubt yourself, Alex, but don't doubt me.'

'You're my one constant and I can't risk losing that. Not again.' She reached up with her other hand, cupping his cheek, drinking him in. 'I do love you, Finn. I have loved you my whole life. I love your heart and your soul, your courage and your kindness. I love watching you with the girls and seeing how safe they are with you looking out for them.

I love your vision for Hawk and the company you've built. I love what you are doing at Blakeley and knowing that my ancestors are respected by you. I love you. If I loved you less I might take a risk. But you deserve more. Your girls deserve more. Let me do the right thing, Finn. Let me go.'

Standing on her toes, she pressed a soft kiss to his mouth, trying to imprint every sensation on her memory: his scent, his taste, the way his mouth felt, firm and yet so tender. She tasted salt and didn't know who was crying, him or her.

'Be happy,' she whispered against his mouth, then turned and walked away.

CHAPTER THIRTEEN

'EMILIA, WHAT ARE you doing here?' Alex jumped up from her office chair to embrace her friend. 'It's so good to see you. But I thought you were in Armaria?'

Alex had been home for a day and a half, but the townhouse wasn't quite the sanctuary it usually was. Amber was busy with a series of corporate Christmas parties, Harriet was auditing another company's administrative procedures before heading straight to Rio de Janeiro, and Emilia had gone to Armaria at the weekend to spend a few days with her father and his family, who had recently relocated there, before her stay at the palace.

This meant Alex had been home alone most of the time, as the receptionist they'd employed a couple of months ago, when they'd realised they needed someone full-time in the office had taken annual leave. The townhouse had never felt so empty. It felt a little like purgatory.

They'd worked so hard to make it a home as well as an office space, knocking down the wall between the sitting and dining room to create a welcoming office and reception area, where the wooden floorboards shone with a warm, golden glow, and the original tiled fireplaces had been renovated to shining glory. Two comfortable-looking sofas sat opposite each other at the front of the room, an inviting space for potential clients or staff to relax in, and the receptionist's desk was on the wall behind.

Their own desks, an eclectic mixture of vintage and modern classic, faced the reception area in two rows, with paperwork neatly filed in the shelves built into the alcoves by the back fireplace. Flowers and plants softened the space, and there was a warm floral print on the blinds and curtains, the same theme picked up in the pictures hanging on the walls.

The door at the back led to a narrow kitchen and a sunny conservatory extension that they used as a sitting-cum-dining room, and they each had a bedroom on the first or second floor—two to a floor, sharing a bathroom.

Cosy for four, it was too big a house for one person.

Alex gave Emilia a quick hug. Neither was a demonstrative woman, but they had grown closer during the summer, when Alex had helped Emilia organise the Armarian Midsummer Ball and encouraged her to tell Laurent how she felt about him.

'You do know it's Christmas Eve, right? You *are* supposed to be in Armaria.'

'I came back because we always spend Christmas Eve together,' said Emilia. 'So put the "out of office" on, switch the phones to "off". No one is going to need anyone at midday on Christmas Eve. Let's go. The car is coming to whisk me back to the airport at four, so we have all afternoon.'

'It's so good to see you.'

Alex swallowed the lump in her throat, blinking back threatening tears. She was the calm and collected one. She never cried, never had emotional crises. She didn't intend to start now, but she hadn't realised how much she needed to see her friends.

Pulling on her coat and grabbing her bag, Alex followed Emilia out of the house into the cold, crisp day. The snow was gone from the London streets, but the temperature was still below zero, the railings and bare tree branches glistening with frost despite the winter sun.

They didn't walk far. Emilia stopped at the small wine bar and restaurant at the top of their street, where they often went for an after-work drink or weekend brunch.

'After you,' she said.

Alex pushed the door and walked into the dimly lit restaurant. Only to stop in surprise, feeling something as close to happiness as she had felt over the last few days rushing through her.

'Harry! Aren't you in Rio? What's going on? Amber—lovely to see you.'

'It's like I said,' Emilia said, squeezing her hand. 'It's Christmas Eve and we spend it together. Harry and I are going to the airport together at four. I'll be in Armaria by six—'

'And I'll land in Rio tomorrow morning, so I'll be with Deangelo and his family for Christmas.' Harriet enfolded Alex in a hug. 'How could I miss our Christmas Eve?'

'And you and I will go for our usual walk tomorrow.' Amber smiled at Emilia as the waiter brought a bottle of champagne over to their table and expertly opened it. 'But first we deserve a Christmas party of our own. We've all worked so hard this year.'

Alex had never told them that Christmas

Eve was her birthday, nor how much she appreciated their tradition of meeting up and spending the day together. And yet somehow they knew she needed them. She wasn't as alone as she thought; even with all the changes on the horizon they were still a team.

It had been far too long since all four of them had been together, and the next couple of hours passed quickly as they sipped their champagne and ate a delicious assortment of tapas.

By common assent they decided against talking about work for a while, which meant Alex didn't have to talk about Finn or Blakeley. Instead she listened as the other three discussed their Christmas plans.

Emilia immediately invited Amber and Alex to Armaria when she heard they were planning to book a last-minute deal for the week.

'I should have thought before,' she said remorsefully. 'Of course I'm a guest, both at Dad's and at the palace, so it's not really my place to invite people, but it's not fair for Harry and I to be away and leave you two alone. Laurent won't mind. I'll text him. There's great skiing; you ski, don't you, Alex?'

This would be the perfect time to mention

that she'd been in Austria at the weekend, but Alex had no words to touch upon what had happened there. Instead she just nodded and applied herself to her barely touched plate.

The discussion quietened and when she looked up all three of her friends were staring at her.

'What is it?'

'You've been quiet, even for you.'

'And you came back early from your last job and didn't say why.'

'Alex, you look so sad. Please let us help.' Amber spoke last as she covered Alex's hand with hers.

Alex inhaled breath, long and painful, thoughts tumbling around her head. If she told them who she was—what she really was—those words could never be taken back. But she was so tired of carrying secrets.

She stared at her still full plate, her barely touched glass, and felt her resistance shatter into tiny pieces. She couldn't be this alone any more. She just couldn't. And if she didn't let in these girls, these amazing resilient women, then she was doomed for sure.

She looked up at the three concerned faces and tried to summon a smile. 'My name isn't Alex,' she said slowly. 'At least it is now, but

I was born Lola Beaumont and I grew up at Blakeley Castle.'

'But isn't that where you've just been?' Emilia asked.

Alex nodded.

Amber's hand tightened on hers. 'It must have been very difficult,' she said softly.

And the sympathy in her voice and in the faces of all three of her friends undid Alex. She couldn't stop the tears gathering in her eyes and falling down her face as she finally told them it all. Every detail of who she was, what had happened—and about Finn.

'Here's your tea.'

Amber handed Alex a steaming mug and Alex accepted it gratefully. They were all back at the house, with Alex placed firmly on the sofa with a blanket and told not to get up.

'Your Finn sounds like a hottie!' Harriet had her phone in front of her and now she squealed, holding it up so they could all see the picture she'd found of Finn, looking rugged, surfboard in hand. 'Oh, he *is*! Tall, dark and handsome—just the way I like them.'

'And you an engaged woman,' Amber scolded her.

Harriet laughed. 'Deangelo knows I love him completely, but that doesn't mean I can't appreciate a good-looking man when I see one. But, more importantly, he sounds kind. Looking after his nieces the way he does is a wonderful thing, and Hawk has a great reputation as an employer and for its ethos.'

'He is kind,' Alex said. 'He's a very good man.'

And hot too, she silently agreed.

'In fact...' Harriet smiled at her. 'He sounds like a keeper. Alex, why are you here with us and not with him?'

It was a very good question.

'I told you. He needs a stable person for the girls. Not someone who has no idea who she really is.'

'A very wise person once said something to me and I've never forgotten it,' Emilia said, perching on the sofa next to Alex. 'She said: "If the worst comes to the worst we're here for you. We're your family. We'll pick you up and heal you. But going through life too scared to put yourself out there isn't living, it's existing, and you deserve more. We all do." *You* told me that this summer, and you were right. Living fully is scary, Alex. It's much easier to sleepwalk through life. But it sounds to me like Finn woke you up. It's up to you what you do with your life now, but do you really want any more regrets?'

'It's easy to be wise for other people,' Alex said, but her own words, repeated back to her, resonated through her. 'It's not just me. It's the girls, it's being found out again, it's being Lola once more, and the press...' She shivered. 'If they're going to find me I can't bring that to their door.'

'So you're going to hole up here and withstand the siege?' Harriet asked.

'I'm hoping there won't be a siege, but, yes. What else can I do?'

'What would you tell me to do if I was in your position?' Amber asked, pulling up a chair to sit opposite, her large green eyes fixed firmly on Alex. 'I've a secret and there's a good chance it might be discovered. I don't know if the press will descend tonight, or tomorrow, or next week. All I know is that I am going to spend the next few weeks, months, years in fear. What would you tell me to do?'

'I'd tell you to own it,' Alex said reluctantly.

'How?'

'I... I would tell you to get your side out first. To find a friendly journalist and offer an exclusive. And to pick a time of year when the news cycles are busy to minimise the exposure.'

'Like Christmas?'

'Like Christmas...'

Amber didn't say anything else. She just waited. Harriet and Emilia sat still and silent as Alex stared at her tea. Amber was absolutely right. Her advice was always to own the story, to control as much of the narrative as possible. And yet here she was, allowing the narrative of her life to be controlled by fear, by what might happen. Finn was right too. Lola would have laughed at the headlines, turned them to her advantage. Alex was hiding from them.

What if there were a middle way? And, more importantly, if there was, was she brave enough to take it?

A phone beeped, breaking the silence, and Emilia got to her feet, pressing a light kiss to Alex's head. 'The car is here and Harry and I need to go. It would be lovely to see you and Amber in Armaria, so let me know if you're coming. But if I were you I'd be on my way to another castle. Think about it, Alex. Merry Christmas, Amber.'

'I'll see you both soon. Have a wonderful Christmas.' Harriet threw her arms around first Amber and then Alex.

The two women left in a flurry of hugs, kisses and 'Merry Christmases', leaving Amber and Alex alone in the darkening kitchen, looking at each other.

'You know what I really want for Christmas?' Amber said. 'A nativity scene. Any idea where we can see one?'

Alex stared at her. Could she do it? Go to Blakeley and know she would certainly be unmasked, sooner or later. Risk finding happiness knowing it could end at any time, that there were no guarantees? But, more importantly, could she *not*? She'd thought there were no second chances. Not for her. But fate—and Finn—had shown her the possibility of a different life. All that was stopping her from taking it was fear. And she was so tired of being afraid.

'It's a good thing I know where there is one. Pack your bag, Amber, we have an invitation to a castle this Christmas. But first,' she said, resolution filling her, 'I have a phone call to make.'

CHAPTER FOURTEEN

'ALEX PROMISED SHE'D be here.' Scarlett's lower lip wobbled dangerously.

Finn knew how she felt. He still couldn't believe Alex had packed her bags and left that very night in Austria. No backward look. Uncaring of who she left behind. Again.

Heaving a sigh, Finn pulled at one of the woolly ears adorning Scarlett's head. 'She'd be here if she could, Scar. It's not her fault she has to work.'

'No one has to work on Christmas Eve apart from Father Christmas and his elves. Oh, and vicars.'

'Lots of people work over Christmas. Come on, let's get you backstage. Can you imagine the disaster if we didn't hear your "baa" at the right moment? The whole play would be ruined.'

Finn watched Scarlett prance ahead. She was never down for too long. She looked adorable in her white fleecy costume with its little woolly tail and pointy ears—and he had no one to share the moment with.

His sister should be here—he'd sent her an invitation and offered to pay her plane fare from wherever she was, but Nicky hadn't replied. He didn't know if it was a good or bad sign that the girls never asked about their mother, and nor did they expect to see her. But they did want to see Alex. The thing he had promised himself never to let them do had happened: they had got attached to someone temporary.

And they weren't the only ones. It wasn't Nicky he wanted next to him, much as he hoped she'd make an appearance for the girls' sake, he wanted to share this moment with Alex.

The real question, the question which had been nagging at him for the past two days, was what he was going to do about it. Should he respect Alex's wish to live a quiet, safe life or do what he wished he'd done ten years ago and go after her? Show her he was hers, always?

So far he hadn't had any enquiries about the identity of his temporary PR manager. Maybe Sofia had believed Alex when she'd denied any prior acquaintance, but the truth was bound to come out one day. Wouldn't it be better for her to be with people who loved her when that happened? Wouldn't it be better for her to be with people who loved her whatever the future held? Shouldn't that be how everyone lived?

He looked around the ballroom, filled with laughing, chattering people. It was as unlike the Beaumonts' famously decadent Christmas Eve parties as a party could be. Instead of the great and the good, the famous and curious, he'd invited the whole village, owners of local businesses and neighbours, plus all his staff, with coaches laid on to take them back to London and Reading and a shuttle bus prepared to do several station runs for those wanting to catch trains back to family. Some people had come dressed up, others were in jeans. There was no dress code, no expectation., All he wanted was to see the ballroom full of seasonal cheer.

At one end of the ballroom a buffet table groaned under the weight of food, while waiters and waitresses circulated with canapés and trays of drinks. A kids' bar and buffet were in the attached dining hall, along with paid entertainers, to give the adults a chance to relax and their over-excited offspring an opportunity to work off their Christmas Eve energy.

Finn had also arranged for a TV to be set up, with rows of comfortable chairs and bean-bags, and a selection of kids Christmas films ready to go. After the nativity play and some carols, the children would have their own party while a band entertained the adults, and the whole thing would finish at eleven to give those who wanted to attend Midnight Mass time to get there.

He'd been planning the event for months. It was his statement as the new owner of the castle, ushering in a new era. He should feel pride at its success, but instead he was just desperately tired. He felt as if he'd let Alex down all over again, that he should have found the right words to make her trust in him, in them.

But if telling her he loved her weren't the right words then he wasn't sure what they were. Would she ever be ready to accept love? Would it ever be their time?

With a start he realised that the small stage set at one end of the ballroom was filling with children and that people were beginning to sit in the rows of chairs placed in front. The school choir stood to one side, self-important in their smart cassocks, and the orchestra was nervously tuning up next to them. Right at the front of the stage, standing to one side, was Saffy, white with nerves, biting her lip.

Finn held a hand up to attract her attention, giving her a grin and a thumbs-up when he had it.

He wanted his nieces to be the best they could be, not to be afraid to love or to go after what they wanted. Didn't he owe it to them to set a good example? Didn't he owe it to himself?

He still had Alex's Christmas tree ornament in his pocket, like a talisman. He should go and give it to her. Tell her he was here for her whenever she needed him. That this time he wasn't going to just watch her walk away. It was up to her what she did with the information, but at least she would know.

Mind made up, Finn strode to a seat at the back, phone out, ready to record Scarlett's big moment, having promised Saffy not to embarrass her with as much as a photo.

As he sat down the orchestra began to play the first strains of 'Once in Royal David's City', and a boy with a cheeky smile and tousled hair sang the first verse with a voice of such sweet power Finn could hardly credit someone so small could manage it. The rest of the choir joined in and then, blushing furiously, Saffy spoke.

'Once upon a time there was a woman named Mary, and she lived in a place called Nazareth...'

Her voice shook at first, but grew steadier as she went on. He could see the relief on her face when the girl playing Mary delivered her first line and attention switched to the actors.

It was the most traditional of traditional nativities. No whales or dinosaurs at this manger. But it had a simplicity that appealed to Finn, with the old carols threading through the narrative, the whole audience joining in with a gusto that clearly amazed the vicar. Finn sat still, proudly blinking back tears as Saffy, her confidence growing with every word, narrated beautifully.

And then his absorption was broken by low voices and a clatter by the door next to him.

He looked round, annoyed, as the door opened and the sound of high heels announced the entrance of newcomers, their attempts to walk quietly almost comical, before switching his attention back to the stage, vaguely aware that two figures had stopped behind him.

At that moment a spotlight highlighted the back of the hall, in readiness for the shepherds to walk down the aisle, and he heard Saffy let out a peculiar little cry, half-sob, half-unintelligible word, her face shining with shock and happiness as she gazed at the spotlight.

Finn twisted round to see what she was looking at and it was all he could do not to repeat his niece's cry.

It was Alex.

Happiness burst through his body, through his very soul at the sight. He didn't need to go and find her. She had returned to him.

To them.

'Hey…' he whispered.

'Hey.'

At that moment the shepherds ushered their small flock into the back of the hall, ready to be dazzled by an angel on the stage, only for one lamb to utter a loud cry and break away from the herd to fling itself at Alex.

Finn looked at Alex as she bent down and enfolded the lamb in her arms, meeting his gaze with her own steady one. And he knew for certain. She'd come back for them all. For good.

'Okay, girls. Go and get some food and let Alex and her friend get a drink and some food of their own. It's lovely to meet you,'

Finn said to Amber. 'I'm so pleased you are joining us for Christmas.'

'You're really staying for Christmas?' Scarlett asked, still in her lamb costume.

Alex nodded. 'If that's okay with you two?'

'Yes!' Scarlett nodded so enthusiastically her ears were in danger of coming off.

Saffron's smile was more sedate, but her dark eyes shone and Alex gave her a gentle hug.

'You were brilliant. I'm sorry we were so late; it was hard getting a taxi at Reading station.'

'That's okay,' Saffy said. 'I'm glad you're here. Come on, Scar. Otherwise only the yucky sandwiches will be left.'

Alex watched the two girls run off to the dining room, taking in the ballroom as she did so. Christmas Eve at Blakeley, a party. Just like old times. A band up on stage, people milling and talking and laughing. But this was a family occasion—a community event. If people were drinking to excess or taking drugs or engaging in affairs and dares then she couldn't see it. Everyone looked festive, many in party clothes, but no one was in haute couture, costing enough to feed a family for a year, or dripping in diamonds. Her ancestors would probably think it a tame affair, but she liked the simplicity of it.

She knew people were watching her, trying to figure out who she was. Some had noticed her in the last two weeks, but many of the villagers hadn't seen her at all while she'd been working there; she'd done her best to stay out of sight of the village.

With her hair down, and wearing a severely cut black cocktail dress, she knew she looked more like Lola than she had done during her whole stay at Blakeley. It was likely someone would recognise her sooner rather than later. But that was okay.

Alex inhaled, nerves fluttering. With Finn by her side she could handle it.

'I'm going to get some food,' Amber said, touching her arm reassuringly. 'And Saffy tells me that the first film scheduled is *The Muppets Christmas Carol*. So, much as I'm looking forward to the band, I might join the kids for a bit. I can't resist that film.'

Dear Amber. Subtly telling Alex that she was okay and would be fine by herself. 'Have fun.'

Amber's green eyes sparkled. 'You too.'

'Would you like a drink?' Finn smiled down at her and Alex's stomach flipped with nerves mingled with desire.

'You're in a suit again? This is becoming a habit.'

'You look beautiful,' he said softly, and her desire ramped up, painful in its intensity.

'Thank you. Can we go for a walk? I need some air.'

And to talk without everyone surreptitiously watching them.

'Sure.'

Finn guided her out of the ballroom and back through to the west wing, so they could slip out through the side door, avoiding all the other people getting some cool air after the heat of the ballroom, stopping only to collect their coats to guard against the winter chill.

Alex took a deep breath, feeling the shock of what she had just done enfolding her. 'I called a journalist. A feature writer I've known a while. She's fair. I trust her to be fair. I am going to meet her back in London on Boxing Day and give her the story—all of it.'

Finn took her hand, his fingers warm and strong and comforting. 'Tell her to come here.'

'Finn...'

'Blakeley is embedded in you, in your story. You should tell it here. I want to be with you this time.'

Relief flooded her, and the tension she'd

held since making the call melted away. 'I'd like that.'

'You're very brave. I'm proud of you.'

'It was Amber. She made me see that I was ignoring my own best advice, letting the story rule me, not me it. I'm not brave— I am quite frankly terrified—but it's time. How can I have a future if I'm hiding from the past?' She looked out across the moonlit landscape. 'Would you mind if we walked to the lake?'

He raised an eyebrow in surprise. He must have noticed how she had avoided the lake over the last few weeks, but if she was going to do this, be here, there were a few more ghosts to lay to rest first.

The path was lit by lanterns, the same lanterns as those hanging in trees around the castle, and the moon was hidden by low clouds. It smelt like snow.

Finn took her hand as they neared the lake and Alex entwined her fingers with his, glad of his strength. Finally they reached the low platform bordering the lake. The same platform she had fished from, launched boats from and swum from summer after summer. She stepped onto it, looking out into the dark, inky depths, thinking of the young woman who had died there exactly ten years ago and in doing so had set in chain a series of events which had totally changed Alex's life.

'She was high,' she said after a while. 'So out of it that she thought it was a good idea to swim in the lake on Christmas Eve night. The inquest said that if she hadn't drowned she would probably have died of hypothermia. Dad realised she was missing and came to find her. He pulled her body out of the lake. She was only twenty-three, did you know that? Meanwhile my mother was sleeping with that girl's husband back at the castle. We thought normal rules didn't apply to us, that we were somehow above it all. But we were so wrong. And that poor young woman paid the price. Kate paid the price.'

She hadn't spoken the name for years, and doing so now lifted a weight from her heart she had been carrying for so long she'd forgotten it was there.

'And my dad. I never knew whether he was taking the coward's way out or whether he truly thought he was doing the right thing. I've always wondered if he thought about me at all...'

Finn held her close, his clasp firm and reassuring. 'You are not your parents. What happened here was tragic, and it was desperately sad, but it shouldn't define you. You can't let it define you any more. I told you. I don't care if you call yourself Alex or Lola or anything else. Names are just words. What matters is what is in here.' Finn touched his chest. 'You have a good heart. That's what matters. And you have *my* heart, whatever you want to do with it. It's yours.'

He reached into his pocket and brought out a small paper bag.

'I didn't get a chance to wrap it...sorry. Happy Birthday, Alex.'

She recognised the logo on the bag. It was from the glass shop in Austria, where she'd bought the girls' necklaces, now both wrapped and in her bag ready for the morning. Opening it, she saw a tissue-wrapped object. She slowly pulled it from the bag, unwrapping the tissue to reveal an exquisite crystal Christmas tree ornament—a heart.

She held it up to the lantern light, watching the light sparkle off it. 'It's beautiful.'

'Will you take it, Alex? Will you take my heart? I come with a lot of baggage, I know. Memories you want to forget and two pre-teen girls and a castle full of your ancestors. But I love you. I always have. I want to be by your side no matter what life throws at you. You think you need to be alone. You don't. I'm here. I'll always be here.'

Alex looked at the crystal heart a little longer, her own heart too full for her to find words. Then, slipping it into her pocket, she reached out and took Finn's hand, drawing him away from the lake. She looked back at the lake for one long moment and felt the last ghost slip into its depths.

She waited to speak until they were halfway along the path, drawing him close to her under a tree, looking at the castle lit up against the snow-heavy sky.

'I'm scared,' she said honestly. 'Scared that I'll let you down, that I'll let the girls down. Scared that one day you'll wake up and realise I'm not enough. It's almost overwhelming. It's as if I pushed all that fear deep down and hid it, along with every other emotion. That I survived by not feeling and not living, by being asleep in my own life. And then you fought your way back into my life and woke me up, and it's been more painful and harder than I could ever have imagined. But also more wonderful. You, the girls, being back here at Blakeley... It's like all the wishes I never dared to dream have come true. And it's all thanks to you. My knight, the only person who has always seen me. I can't believe you love me. I can't believe I get to be that lucky. I have always loved you, Finn. Always.'

'I know you have your business, and your life in London, and I know you have huge ambition and that's part of what I love about you,' Finn said hoarsely. 'But we can make it work. You can have your own offices here or commute. Whatever you need. All I know is that if you agree to give this a go then I won't be stupid enough to let you walk away a third time.'

'I can't believe that I can be this lucky. That I get to have my agency and my friends, you and the girls and Blakeley. There were so many times when I never thought I'd be happy again. But you do know, don't you, that Hawk and Blakeley don't change anything? I'd want to be with you and the girls no matter where you lived or what you did. Being able to come home is just the cherry on the cake, but you're the cake.'

Finn gave a sudden shout of laughter at her words, his expression turning serious as he gazed down at her. 'Welcome home, Alex.'

He bent to kiss her and she reached for him, entwining her arms around his neck, pressing so close to him she could feel every sinew and muscle, feel the beat of his heart in time with hers.

As his mouth found hers the snow began to fall, settling in her hair, on her arms and shoulders, but she was warm within his arms, warmed by his embrace.

'Merry Christmas,' she whispered against his mouth, and felt him smile.

'Merry Christmas, my love.'

* * * * *

*If you missed the previous stories in
the Fairytale Brides quartet,
check out*

Honeymooning with Her Brazilian Boss
Cinderella's Secret Royal Fling

*And look out for the next book
Coming soon!*

*If you enjoyed this story,
check out these other great reads
from Jessica Gilmore*

Summer Romance with the Italian Tycoon
Baby Surprise for the Spanish Billionaire

Available now!